HD.

"You kno... I could h... you..."

He was unreadable. "From your father and your ex-husband's point of view, they see no reason why they shouldn't bully you into returning to the marriage they arranged."

"So?"

"So attach yourself to me," Rupert advised. "Oh, don't look like that. I'm not suggesting anything irreversible. Just a brief public affair." He gave an ironic laugh. "I'm peculiarly well qualified, as far as publicity goes."

"I can't. I don't like affairs." In a rush of desperation she added, "I don't like sex—it was one of my husband's chief complaints. And I don't suppose I'll change now."

"I see," he said slowly, as if he'd just been presented with an interesting problem. Then he flashed her a disarming grin. "We can still tell the papers we're having an affair without making it true. Of course, it's not as much fun...."

SOPHIE WESTON wrote and illustrated her first book—at the age of five. After university she decided on a career in international finance, which was tremendously stimulating and demanding, but it was not enough. Something was missing in her life, and that something turned out to be writing. These days her life is complete. She loves exciting travel and adventure yet hates to stray too long from her homey cottage in Chelsea, where she writes.

Books by Sophie Weston

These books may be available at your local bookseller.

Don't miss any of our special offers. Write to us at the following address for information on our newest releases.

Harlequin Reader Service
901 Fuhrmann Blvd., P.O. Box 1397, Buffalo, NY 14240
Canadian address: P.O. Box 603,
Fort Erie, Ont. L2A 5X3

SOPHIE WESTON

yesterday's mirror

Harlequin Books

TORONTO • NEW YORK • LONDON
AMSTERDAM • PARIS • SYDNEY • HAMBURG
STOCKHOLM • ATHENS • TOKYO • MILAN

Harlequin Presents first edition February 1987
ISBN 0-373-10957-1

Original hardcover edition published in 1986
by Mills & Boon Limited

Copyright © 1986 by Sophie Weston. All rights reserved.
Philippine copyright 1986. Australian copyright 1986.
Except for use in any review, the reproduction or utilization of
this work in whole or in part in any form by any electronic,
mechanical or other means, now known or hereafter invented,
including xerography, photocopying and recording, or in any
information storage or retrieval system, is forbidden without
the permission of the publisher, Harlequin Enterprises Limited,
225 Duncan Mill Road, Don Mills, Ontario, Canada M3B 3K9.

All the characters in this book have no existence outside the
imagination of the author and have no relation whatsoever to
anyone bearing the same name or names. They are not even
distantly inspired by any individual known or unknown to the
author, and all incidents are pure invention.

The Harlequin trademarks, consisting of the words
HARLEQUIN PRESENTS and the portrayal of a Harlequin,
are trademarks of Harlequin Enterprises Limited and are
registered in the Canada Trade Marks Office; the portrayal
of a Harlequin is registered in the United States Patent
and Trademarks Office.

Printed in U.S.A.

CHAPTER ONE

'So what's he like?' demanded Lesley Button with avidity, almost before the door was shut upon them.

For a moment Cressida did not answer. She was watching the chauffeur ease himself into the front seat of the limousine and adjust his cap. He turned the key and the highly tuned engine sighed into life. Cressida touched a switch beside her and the sound-proof partition which her father had insisted on slid smoothly up between the driver and his passengers.

She relaxed at last, stretching her legs out into the luxurious space in front of her.

'The aeroplane was cramped,' she remarked. 'I feel like one of those uncrushable dresses that could do with a good shaking out.'

Her secretary had no patience with this inconsequentiality.

'Don't change the subject. What's he *like*?'

Cressida turned weary eyes on her in faint amusement. Her secretary was very little younger than herself—indeed, they were very good companions as a result—but she retained the enthusiasm of a schoolgirl. After three days of non-stop negotiations and a particularly rough transatlantic flight, it made Cressida feel pale.

She told Lesley so, with a wry laugh. 'I'll tell you anything you want to know,' she added, 'only for God's sake don't bounce like that,' as Lesley sat forward eagerly, 'or I shall probably do what I managed not to do in the plane, and throw up.'

Lesley grinned. 'The trouble with you is you don't appreciate your luck,' she said blithely. 'Travelling the

world, staying in the best hotels, courted by the world's
financiers, dining with the most dashing bachelor in the
universe . . .'

Cressida shut her eyes. 'And that's just tonight,' she
agreed politely. 'Who knows what excitements tomorrow may bring?' She opened her eyes and gave her
secretary a long look. 'You want to change places?'

Lesley wrinkled her nose. 'Well, maybe a little,' she
temporised. 'I'd take dinner with Rupert Dearham any
day of the week,' she offered.

'Nope.' Cressida shook her copper head decisively.
'No partitioning. You take the whole package or
nothing.'

Lesley flung up her hands. 'Oh, well, in that case, no
deal. I've got a private life to think of.'

'Quite,' agreed Cressida with irony. 'Talking of
which, how is he?'

'Promoted,' said Lesley in a tone of quiet satisfaction.
'And talking of marriage at last.'

'Oh.' Cressida was surprised though she took care
not to show it. Lesley had been going out for nearly two
years with an ambitious executive who was more often
out of the country than in it. His movements were
unpredictable and Lesley's life had been a succession of
broken dates and empty evenings. Cressida, recognising
the condition, had been silently sympathetic, hoping
that eventually Lesley would grow out of her
infatuation as she herself had done. Though she had
done it too late, of course. Now she tried to hide her
dismay, saying, 'Well, congratulations.'

Lesley was not deceived. 'Marriage isn't a bad thing
in itself, you know, Cress. Some people even enjoy it.'

Cressida shrugged. 'Sure. I guess I'm just not much
of an advertisement for it, that's all.' She moved her
shoulders, as if the gesture would shake off the bad
memories. 'Don't pay any attention to me, Lesley. Jet-
lag makes me grumpy.'

Lesley's eyes danced. 'Even with the prospect of dining with Rupert Dearham ahead of you? Why, half London would give its eye-teeth to change places with you. The female half,' she added conscientiously.

'And they would be welcome, with or without the exchange of teeth,' returned Cressida. 'All I want is a bath and bed with a good book.'

'You,' Lesley informed her in a tone of outrage, 'are blasée. Oh, come on, Cress,' she added, 'don't be mean. Tell all. Is he as handsome as the pictures? And they say he's terribly charming. Did you lose your heart?'

'There's nothing to tell,' said Cressida, ticking off her answers on the fingers of her gloved hand. 'Handsome—yes. Charming—probably, though not, so far, to me. And no, no heart-loss.'

Lesley eyed her narrowly. 'Yet you catch an earlier flight back from New York in order to have dinner with him?'

Cressida lowered her eyes demurely. 'Business,' she said sweetly, 'is business.' Her lashes lifted and Lesley saw the gleam of mischief that very few people were privileged to see. 'My Papa set it up while I was taking a shower some time round about 2 a.m. New York time yesterday.'

'No!' Lesley was stunned.

The look of amusement deepened. 'Are you surprised?'

'Maybe not at your father,' admitted Lesley who had worked in London when Jerome Sebastian was still running the UK operation himself and knew a good deal about his imperious temper as a result 'But Lord Dearham is another story. Surely Mr Sebastian can't order *him* around.'

'No,' agreed Cressida with irony. 'That's why I'm to give the man dinner this evening. Since my father has blown it by trying to bully the man, I am to overwhelm him with tact and diplomacy. And a bigger offer,' she added cynically. 'Always provided, of course, that I don't fall asleep on him first.'

'Oh, what a shame,' said Lesley, genuinely upset. 'When I got your telex about tonight's dinner party, I thought you must have lost your heart to him.'

Cressida looked at her in surprise. 'Did you? But you know I never entertain my personal friends in the London flat. It's the company's and I only use it for company parties. I wouldn't take any man there just because I was in love with him—in that unlikely eventuality.'

'In that unlikely eventuality,' Lesley mimicked, 'you'd take him to the nearest room where you could shut the door on the world: and the hell with who paid the rent.'

Cressida looked unconvinced. 'If you say so. But in this case, I'm afraid, it's strictly business. Lord Dearham said he had to fly back to London and we could talk about it there, since my father would not accept that the discussions in New York were the end of the matter. Papa—or so I am told, as I say, I wasn't actually present—said that I would be here tonight and Lord Dearham must dine with me in Park Square. From what I can gather, the man was running late anyway and would have missed his plane if he'd stayed to argue.' She shrugged. 'So he said yes.' She sent Lesley another teasing look. 'If that sounds to you like the start of a great romance, then you're even more of an optimist than Papa.'

'No,' agreed Lesley, sighing. 'No, I have to admit that it doesn't.'

Cressida chuckled suddenly. 'Don't look so disappointed. It would be much worse if it were the start of a big romance.'

'Oh, Why?'

'You know his reputation as well as I do,' Cressida said calmly. 'A wild affair—champagne, diamonds and lots of stories in the newspapers—and three months later he's going up the Amazon or over the North Pole leaving the lady in the case with just her press cuttings and her diamond bracelets to keep her warm. You wouldn't really wish that on me, would you, Lesley? A champagne hangover and a broken heart?'

Her voice was light, mocking, but there was an undercurrent of pain that Lesley knew her too well either to mistake or to refer to.

'You wouldn't break your heart,' she said. 'You're not like those silly girls he usually sees.'

'No?' Cressida looked out of the window, carefully keeping her face averted from Lesley's perceptive eyes. 'I don't think any of us are very different from any of the rest when a man walks out on us. I guess you'd say we were all silly,' she said in a brittle voice. 'I've seen it happen too often—and not just to me. Believe me, men like Rupert Dearham are worth keeping away from.'

Lesley was moved to protest. 'You can't say that. You hardly know him. Just because you've had meetings about Sebastians taking over his company, it doesn't give you the right to pronounce on his whole character.'

'Right?' Cressida considered it. 'No, perhaps not. But it gives me a reason to think very hard about the man. And you will allow that I have a right to protect myself, I suppose.'

Lesley was curious. 'You feel you need to protect yourself from Rupert Dearham?'

Cressida suppressed a shudder.

'Every woman needs to protect herself from men like Rupert Dearham,' she said soberly. 'They can do a lot of damage.'

She thought about him as she had first seen him at that negotiating table in New York. He was very tall and loose-limbed with a quantity of shining fair hair. He was very tanned, too, as befitted an explorer, she supposed. He had looked tough and strongly muscled compared with all the other men in the room.

Cressida had shivered when their eyes met. Not that he had appeared to be interested in her. She had never seen such blank indifference, in spite of his ingrained courtesy.

She had wondered afterwards what that little shiver of hers had meant. It had almost been like a tremor of awareness, even reluctant attraction, as if she had recognised a long-expected intruder into her life. The thought had distracted her. She had had to put it away firmly in order to concentrate on the discussions that ensued. But every time she looked at Rupert Dearham it was there: like a splinter under the skin she could neither remove nor quite forget.

She had thanked her stars that she was no longer at an impressionable age and that experience had taught her to steer clear of men, all men, or she could have been hankering after Lord Dearham in very little time. And that would have been disastrous.

Lesley said slowly, 'You mean you felt he threatened you?'

Cressida repudiated the suggestion hastily. She knew how her secretary deplored her single life and determination not to marry again. She said it was a waste whereas Cressida knew quite well that it was the only way to ensure that she did not break apart, as she so nearly had at the end of her wretched marriage.

'No. Not me personally. But he makes me uneasy in general. He looks like a handsome playboy. He even behaves like one. Of course, he is ridiculously handsome but he has all the other tricks as well. Everything is a joke. He pretends he can't add up to save his life. Claims he can't understand business, he's just a simple explorer.' She hesitated.

'But——' prompted Lesley, intrigued.

'I'm not sure, but I don't trust him. He's too——' she hesitated, '——determined.'

'Determined? On what?'

'He knows his own mind and he sticks to it. You don't expect that in a playboy. Or at least, I don't. There's something almost—well, almost implacable about him. I think,' said Cressida slowly, 'that in some circumstances I might even be frightened of him.'

That startled Lesley. '*Frightened* of him! Why on earth?' A thought occurred to her. 'He didn't try to make a pass at you or anything?' for she knew exactly how Cressida reacted to any indication that a man was interested in her.

But Cressida laughed the idea to scorn. 'We were locked in a smoky room full of puffing lawyers and dehydrating sandwiches,' she assured her secretary. 'It would have been beyond even Lord Dearham's celebrated charm to make any successful passes in that atmosphere, even if he had wanted to, which, as far as I can tell, he didn't. No, it's deeper than that. It's——' she paused, frowning, and then said abruptly, 'he wasn't in the least impressed by Papa. Not the money, not the power, not what he was being offered. He didn't even care when Papa started shouting.'

Lesley, who knew Jerome Sebastian in that mood and had seen the effect it had on subordinates and colleagues alike, shared his daughter's amazement.

'He didn't shout back or anything. Some people do, the ones who stand up to him. But not Lord Dearham. He didn't even try to argue with him. He just sat there—looking rather elegant and bored—and let Papa rant on. And then he said "No". Nothing else. No reasons. No token expression of regret. Just "No". And he wasn't putting on an act, either, I'm sure of it. He was calculating all the time. He came to that meeting not sure what his answer should be and he made up his mind while Papa was trying to bully him. And none of it showed on his face. His eyes didn't change at all.' Cressida looked at Lesley almost in horror, remembering that absolute self-possession. 'And I suppose that's what frightens me—the lack of feeling.'

In spite of herself, Lesley was impressed. She had read the newspapers' version of Lord Dearham's exploits over the years and he sounded, she thought, a charming, lighthearted sort of fellow, just the type of man to shake Cressida out of her routine of work, work and yet more work. In love and happy herself, Lesley Button was more than ever concerned about the lack of affection in her employer's life.

Not, she would have agreed, that Cressida lacked friends though she saw little enough of them, with the hours she worked and the amount of transatlantic hopping she did. Her record on the breaking of dates was not very much better than Lesley's Simon's. But there was no man in her life. No man was every allowed to get near her. It was rumoured in the Sebastian Building that that was due to the influence of old Jerome who wanted to keep his daughter's nose to the grindstone, amassing even more money to be swallowed up by the Jerome coffers.

But Lesley Button knew differently. If there was no man in Cressida's life it was because that was what Cressida had chosen. Even if she had been as ugly as sin and as disagreeable as a wet Sunday there were plenty of men only too happy to wine and dine the heir to the Sebastian millions. And she was neither. Though Lesley would not have admitted it to anyone other than herself, however, she did think that Cressida was unduly sober for her years. After all she was not yet thirty, though she behaved as if she were her father's contemporary and had all the cares of the world on her shoulders beside.

In Lesley Button's view, a little skimming the surface with a practised charmer like Rupert Dearham would have done Cressida a great deal of good. She sighed, recognising that it was out of the question. Cressida had been quite unmistakable on that. And perhaps it was just as well, if he were more than he seemed. Lesley knew, none better, that Cressida would not welcome another calculating businessman in her life. Not after——

'Oh, we're home, said Cressida, interrupting her thoughts. 'I shall have time for a bath, thank God. But only if I hurry. That damned plane was so late ... Look, would you mind if I left you to organise the cases while I dive into the bath? Then help yourself to a drink and come along to my room. You can tell me who else is coming and menus and things while I'm dressing.'

'Right,' said Lesley with composure. She had done such things before on several occasions. Cressida's schedule was often too tight to allow for more than the briefest of showers before she changed. An unexpected travelling delay could throw it out completely. 'You ablute, I'll follow.'

Cressida jumped lightly out of the Rolls with a quick smile of thanks at the chauffeur, and was making for the porticoed entrance.

'Give me ten minutes in the asses' milk,' she said wryly and disappeared.

The chauffeur under Lesley's direction unloaded three matching cases and a battered leather music-case. The briefcases left in the boot she directed him to take direct to the Sebastian Building where he was to leave the Rolls for the night. He looked surprised.

'Am I not to come back here then?'

'No.' Lesley shook her head firmly. 'You're off duty from the moment you check in those briefcases. We're dining here tonight.'

'What, you too?' he asked.

Lesley grinned. The new chauffeurs were often surprised at the friendship between the chief executive and her secretary. Most of them found Cressida too remote to imagine her being informal Or, as old Dicky

Hubert, who had driven Jerome for twenty years, put it, she was too starchy to be real for a girl of her age. Dicky, who had taught her to drive, did not approve of the change in Cressida over the years but Dicky was retired now and Lesley did not often see him these days. So her major source of information on Cressida's life had been removed. Cressida herself never spoke of the past.

Lesley went into the opulent building frowning. There was a key there somewhere, she was sure, somewhere in the past. At some point before Lesley knew her, somebody had done something to Cressida which had made her withdraw from all but the most superficial human contact. In fact, as Lesley had more than once told her, she had locked herself up in an ivory tower and thrown away the key. And if any man was willing to try to climb up and rescue her, she was quite capable of deluging her champion with boiling oil.

Cressida had protested, laughed, and, seeing that Lesley was serious, finally admitted that she was probably right. And, she had added firmly, she was quite happy with the arrangement and would resist strenuously any attempts to dismantle the ivory tower. Lesley had thrown up her hands in frustration. But she had taken the hint. One did not lightly disregard Cressida's expressed intentions.

Lesley took the lift to the Sebastian penthouse, using her key in the security lock. It was a shame, though. Cressida could be so kind, so genuinely sympathetic and—occasionally, when she forgot herself and let her hair down—terrific company. What could it have been that put that coldness in her heart, that hint of tragedy in her eyes? Her father? He was an old monster most of the time but Lesley would have sworn he was genuinely fond of his daughter. Some youthful folly? An old love affair from which she had never recovered? If only she were not so formidable, thought Lesley, unloading cases into the apartment and banishing the lift, one could have asked her.

At that moment the formidable object of her reflections was lying immobile in a warm bath, trying to convince herself that three days' hyperactivity and travelling were soaking away in the scented water. She was not having any great success. Her skin was aching. Her eyes felt prickly with tension and, when she moved her shoulder blades, she could feel the knotted muscles which stubbornly refused to relax.

Damn Rupert Dearham, Cressida thought with concentrated fury. Damn him for not selling the company he patently did not want to Jerome Sebastian who did want it. Damn him for not being bothered to refuse his imperious invitation for this evening. And damn him for looking at her as if she were some prototype of an interesting robot. Damn him most of all for leaving her so flustered that she approached the impending dinner party not with her usual resignation but in an absolute fever of apprehension.

With a slight shock, Cressida realised that her mouth was dry. Was it already true then, literally true, what she had said to Lesley she could imagine as a possibility in some circumstances? Was she *afraid* of Rupert Dearham?

She shook her head, furious with herself, and sank deeper in the water. Relax, she told herself. She began to breathe deeply, carefully in the long even rhythm that she had taught herself. It was almost infallible.

She heard the door to her bedroom open and Lesley's voice.

She lifted her own. 'I'm still in the bath.'

'Good. I'll brew you some tea.' called Lesley. 'You've got half an hour.'

By the time she returned Cressida was standing in front of one of the long cupboards in her room, flicking through racks of clothes with a dissatisfied expression.

By contrast to the silk and velvets on the rails, Cressida was wrapped in a navy blue towelling robe several sizes too large for her and bearing distinct signs of wear on the elbows and lapels.

Lesley grinned. She was used to her employer's helpless impatience with clothes. She put down the small tray she was carrying, with its burden of exquisite china and fragrant tea, and crossed to the cupboards.

'Cocktail length but dressy,' she advised briskly, not waiting for Cressida to speak. 'There are eight of us and only Selina Forest will wear jewels.'

Cressida's harassed look diminished. 'Thank God for that, at least.'

Lesley cast an experienced eye over the wardrobe she knew almost as well as she knew her own. She had bought a good deal of it. Cressida disliked dressing up which she only did as part of her professional life, so she often sent her secretary to the collections to buy for her.

'This,' said Lesley, deciding.

She extracted a dramatic woodland-green blouson in stiff taffeta with slashed sleeves, revealing a lining of shot copper silk, and a high starched white ruff that rose up behind the head in place of a collar. It came with black velvet breeches. Lesley went to the shoe cupboard and emerged with a pair of soft green leather boots, laced up the front, which matched the top.

Cressida looked at them with disfavour. 'That?'

'It makes you look fantastic,' Lesley assured her, shaking out the sleeves, as she slid the plastic cover off the outfit.

'Fantastic is right,' said Cressida gloomily, shaking off the robe and shrugging herself into green taffeta. 'I look like a bit-part player in a science-fiction movie.' She glared at herself momentarily in the mirror before slipping into the breeches and pulling on the boots. 'Still I suppose you're right. You usually are. Who else is coming?'

'The Forests, because Michael said he wanted to see you this evening anyway, so Selina cancelled whatever they were doing tonight. The Quinns, I'm afraid.'

Cressida shrugged, seating herself at her dressing-table and beginning to pin her hair up with expert fingers.

'You can't help it,' she said. 'If you're told to put together a dinner party at twenty-four hours' notice, you have to take what you can get in the way of guests. I think it's pretty amazing you could find anyone at all. Anyway I rather like Jemima.'

Lesley bit her lip. 'Poor woman. They say Sefton has got himself a new woman.'

Cressida's eyes met hers in the mirror. 'Then at least he should be off the drink to some extent. It's when he loses them that you have to worry: he drowns his sorrows in brandy, preferably other people's.' She leant forward to attach a swathe of hair. 'Who's the spare man, then? Could Simon make it for once?'

Lesley shook her head. 'Some sort of aide of Lord Dearham's.' She consulted her list. 'His name is Geoffrey Singer and he is allergic to shellfish.'

Cressida gave a choke of laughter. 'You are a genius among secretaries. Is there anything you don't think of?'

'I do my best,' said Lesley, pleased. 'Do you want to look at the menu?'

Cressida groaned. 'I'm sure it's perfect. Just tell Lucien not to give me much of anything. My stomach still feels as if it is in the middle of yesterday.'

'Right.' Lesley consulted her list. 'And wines. Lucien has opened the claret and there's some Chablis in the fridge but I wondered whether you wanted anything else.' And, as Cressida looked blank, 'Champagne or anything?'

'On the principle of fizzy for fun?' asked Cressida wryly. 'Or fizzy for celebrations? I don't think we'll

have much to celebrate after this evening. My papa may
choose to blind himself but I'm pretty clear that Lord
Dearham would rather make over his publishing
company to a cats' home than sell it to Sebastians. So,
no champagne.'

'If he's so set against it, why do you think he agreed
to come tonight?'

'I wish I knew,' said Cressida slowly. She rotated her
head to make sure that the last curling wisps of hair
were caught up. 'I wish I knew.'

She felt no more assured as she went forward to greet
Rupert Dearham some ten minutes later. Slightly to her
surprise he was the first to arrive. He strolled in behind
Lucien, looking understatedly elegant in a suit of
perfect cut. At once Cressida felt outlandish and
overdressed.

'Lord Dearham, madam,' said Lucien at his most
formal.

'How nice to see you again,' Cressida said with more
politeness than truth.

Rupert Dearham's eyes met hers and she had a nasty
suspicion he knew exactly what she was feeling and was
amused by it.

'Is it? You mean we're not going to talk business?' he
asked mockingly.

Disconcerted by this direct attack, Cressida glared at
him.

'You are not my only guest, Lord Dearham. And I
do not normally discuss business at the dinner table.'

Instead of being crushed as she had intended he
looked, if anything, even more amused.

'Really? Does your father know? It sounds like heresy
to the Sebastian creed to me. I thought you stood ready
to discuss business anywhere: board or bed too, for that
matter.'

Cressida almost gasped. She felt as if he had thrown a
glass of icy water in her face. She strove to keep the

shock out of her eyes, knowing that she had started to tremble and being powerless to stop it. He knows, she thought in bewildered pain, he knows.

The thing she had been trying to put out of her mind, the one thing she had withheld from Lesley for all her frankness in other matters, was the thing that this man had detected. Cressida made a despairing gesture, turning away from him in pure instinct to hide her reaction. She felt helpless, suddenly vulnerable. Tiredness, no longer suppressed, washed over her in a wave. She swayed. She felt stripped and shamed.

With a great effort she turned back to face him, the copper head high. Under the light make-up her face was very pale. At her sides her hands were clenched so tightly that they felt as if they would never unlock.

'I assure you I have no intention of discussing business tonight,' she said in a cool voice.

She met his eyes squarely, realising with a slight shock that they were not grey as she had supposed but an opaque shade somewhere between blue and jade. They were wide set under steep lids now drooping lazily. They were also quite without expression.

Rupert Dearham said charmingly, 'Then I look forward to the evening with increased enthusiasm.'

Cressida's mouth stretched in a meaningless smile.

'I hope you will enjoy yourself,' she said formally and heard with relief the unmistakable sounds of the next arrival.

It was the Quinns and the Forests together. She welcomed them mechanically, pouring and mixing drinks with practised hands, less than half her mind on what she was doing. How could he know? How could he? Did he guess? Surely he could not have overheard her father. He must have been out of the building before Jerome swung round on her with his anger blazing.

For a moment Cressida shut her eyes. She could hear

him so clearly he might have been in the room. He had been furious, of course. He was not used to being outfaced, particularly not by decadent aristocrats whose way of life he despised.

'You're no damned use,' Jerome had yelled at her. 'I don't know what I pay you for. You've no sense, no initiative, no *charm*!'

His American aides had looked embarrassed but resigned. They saw this sort of volcanic activity every day. It was nastier when it was directed at his only daughter but it was nothing exceptional. And the only daughter knew that. She had appeared unmoved by the tirade, collecting her papers quietly, not answering him.

'If you were worth your salt you'd have that gigolo wound round your finger by now,' he had shouted, working himself up into a frenzy of indignation. 'He's supposed to have a weakness for women. You could have done something useful for once, instead of sitting on your backside and taking a salary off me for doing damn all.'

This was so manifestly unfair that even his personal assistants had looked startled and the chief accountant, greatly daring, was moved to protest.

Jerome Sebastian had taken no notice. 'Call yourself a woman?' he had told his daughter with contempt. 'Why, you can't catch a man and when I caught you one, you couldn't even hold on to him.'

The aides had begun to leave rapidly. Jerome was unpredictable but there was a strong possibility that he might, in the morning, resent anyone who had been unlucky enough to hear him abusing his daughter with family secrets. Normally father's and daughter's private life was jealously guarded.

'You could have helped. But no. You stick your nose in the air and won't do a thing. I have to do it all myself. Just as I always do. Well, you listen to me, my girl. I'm tired of keeping you in the lap of luxury while you look down your nose at me. I want that company and you're going to get it for me. Or you're out.'

It was not the first time that her father had threatened to fire her. Cressida normally ignored the threats but he had got her on the raw with his taunts. She forgot that he was ageing, that he was lonely and quite often sick. She forgot that she was all he had in the world. She forgot even what she had learned from childhood: that his temper was ungovernable but that he was always pathetically sorry afterwards if he thought he had wounded her.

So she had raised her head and said coldly, 'And how do you suggest I get it for you?'

She had know what he was going to say before he said it. It was, nevertheless. a shock. She had been silent with outrage as he had said,

'You're a woman, aren't you? Behave like one, for once. Do you good. Forget that bloody ice-maiden act. Go to bed with him.'

CHAPTER TWO

'ARE you all right?'

Cressida gave a little jump, coming back to the present with a start. She found she was staring down at the tray of drinks, her hands stilled on the ice-bucket. The low-voiced query returned her to her task.

'Perfectly, thank you,' she said, adding ice to a Campari soda and swirling the mixture vigorously.

'You don't look it,' said Rupert Dearham bluntly.

He took the drink from her, added a sliver of orange and took it across to Geoff Singer for whom it was intended. Then he came back to her.

'That's everyone. Except you, of course. What are you drinking?'

Cressida removed her glass of clear liquid from under his nose.

'I don't need another, Lord Dearham. I haven't finished this and we'll be eating soon.'

He ignored that, taking the glass away from her and sniffing it.

'Mineral water,' he detected. He gave her an ironic look. 'Trying to keep a clear head, Miss Sebastian?'

'Trying to keep a quiet stomach,' Cressida retorted. 'I've been travelling most of today and it doesn't agree with me.'

He was amused but he also looked surprised. 'You mean you only got back today? I thought you were flying back yesterday, as I was.'

'No,' she said with restraint. 'No. I was supposed to be staying in New York until next week.'

'I see.' He did, too. She could see that. He was as

quick as a jungle cat. 'Until your father issued this
invitation and you had to dash home to set the scene?'

'Exactly,' she agreed.

He looked thoughtful. 'Well, I hope it proves to be
worth it.'

Cressida shrugged, not answering, and took a sip
from her glass. Rupert Dearham looked down at her
consideringly from his great height. She had to tilt her
head to look at him.

He really was devastatingly good-looking, Cressida
decided dispassionately. The strong-boned face was
spare and powerful with an aquiline nose and haughty,
well-marked brows. He did not look like the playboy
that her father called him, or the dilettante that the
press had labelled him. He looked composed, self-
contained and very unapproachable. The jut of his
jawline spoke more of decisiveness than his reputation
suggested. But the cynical mouth was everything and
more that the newspapers had prepared her for.

He was observant too. He had taken in her inspection
and was lazily amused by it. 'You really don't like me,
do you, Miss Sebastian?'

Cressida gave him a sweet false smile. 'I don't have
to, Lord Dearham. And the name is Harley. Mrs Harley.'

The lids drooped lower over his eyes. He seemed to
be studying the whisky in his glass absorbedly.

'Is it now? That's very interesting. I don't see you
wearing a ring.'

Cressida turned her hands over, displaying them.
They were bare of ornament.

'Quite right. Well observed. I don't care for rings.'

The mouth, which was not only cynical but
beautifully moulded, moved in a mocking smile.

'Aren't you afraid that your prejudice might have
you facing prosecution under the Trades Description
Act?' he drawled. 'You shouldn't pass yourself off as
the unattached houri when you're not, you know.'

Cressida lifted a shoulder. 'I am sure you are not interested in the degrees of my attachments, Lord Dearham. And as for the trade description—one only needs to worry about that when the goods are for sale.'

The strange green eyes narrowed, staring into hers with sudden intensity.

'Are you telling me you're not?' He sounded frankly disbelieving.

Cressida felt the colour rise in her cheeks. She kept her head high, furious with herself. She could only hope that in the soft electric light her tan might hide the blush.

'No, I'm not,' she said steadily.

To her relief they were interrupted by Lucien announcing dinner. She thanked the manservant and led the way into the dining-room with a feeling that she had been rescued from an untenable position at the last moment.

The table, in spite of the lack of warning, was beautifully set. The cloth was old linen, turning to cream with age, edged with lace that had been crocheted by Cressida's grandmother. Everything else, though, was modern. Jerome Sebastian had arrived in England from Poland with nothing and there were no heirlooms in any of the Sebastian homes.

Not, thought Cressida, looking around, that this apartment could by any stretch of the imagination be called a home. Jerome had bought it for his own use but he had never lived in it. Cressida had a room here where she kept most of her evening dresses and a few other clothes but she seldom did more than use it to change between engagements. She rarely spent a night here except when she was on her way to or from London airport or, as now, entertaining business acquaintances. She disliked it and always had done.

Jerome had engaged an interior decorator who had attracted his attention entirely because she was some sort of minor middle-European royalty. She had had a passion for Scandinavian design and a very advanced painter with whom she had subsequently set up house. As a result, the furniture was white and silver and deep with cushions, the sculptures in dramatically lit niches were steel and the walls were adorned with enormous canvases in primary colours.

However, Cressida could see that Lucien had done his best with the table. The silver and glass gleamed, there was a magnificent display of white and yellow chrysanthemums on the corner table and, in the centre of the dining-table, candles had been lit in the elegant steel candlesticks.

'Thank you Lucien, it looks terrific,' she said to him in a low voice. 'I hope you and Marthe weren't dreadfully put out.'

He smiled. 'It was a pleasure. We enjoy a challenge. And we don't see enough of you, Miss Cressida. We can stay this evening to clear away if you would like.'

She shook her head. 'No. I've put you out quite enough. Just load up the dishwasher after the second course and go when you've served the sweet and cheese. You can quite easily clear up tomorrow.'

He bowed. 'Very good, madam.'

The meal ordered by Lesley was superb, though Cressida tasted very little of it. For one thing she was not hungry. For another, Lord Dearham, sitting on her right, deprived her of what little appetite she might otherwise have commanded. And on her left Sefton Quinn, in spite of being settled in his new love-life, was drinking heavily.

It was Sefton who, pushing his *crème brûlée* away virtually untouched, lurched on to the subject of divorce.

'Wonderful thing, divorce,' he pronounced with the slightest suggestion of a slur. He repossessed his claret glass and cradled it. 'Best invention of the twentieth century.'

Next to Geoff Singer, Jemima Quinn bit her lip.

Cressida rushed into speech. 'Hardly a twentieth-century invention, Sefton. I believe one or two Roman emperors discovered it first.'

'So it's a luxury. And now it's filtered down to the plebs. It's still the greatest breakthrough in communication since the telephone,' Sefton said belligerently. He took a healthy swig from his glass and replenished it from the decanter. Jemima looked as if she might cry at any moment.

'Communication?' Rupert Dearham asked. 'Surely the reverse?'

Sefton stuck out his jaw. 'You're not married, are you? For total non-communication you want to try marriage, old chap. Then you'd know what you were talking about.' It managed not to be an insult by a hair's breadth.

Rupert Dearham measured him with a long slow look. Cressida found she was holding her breath. Eventually he gave his lazy, charming smile and she relaxed almost visibly against the oval back of her chair.

'Ah, but on divorce I'm an expert. A fourth-generation expert you might say.'

Even Sefton was intrigued. 'How come?'

'Father, grandfather and great-grandfather,' Rupert said coolly. 'Great-grandfather had to go to the House of Lords, too. It wasn't just a matter of a day's outing to the divorce court in those days.'

'Good Lord,' said Sefton blankly.

'Yes, it's become a sort of inherited quirk,' said Rupert Dearham in a casual voice. 'Like being left-handed or tone-deaf.'

This was greeted with general laughter and he smiled round the table. Cressida could make out the slight touch of hysteria in Jemima Quinn's laugh and wondered whether anyone else had done. Was Sefton trying to persuade her to divorce him for his new love? If so, her sympathy was with Jemima. She knew all too well how painful that could be.

She said swiftly, trying to keep the conversation away from the Quinns' problems, 'That must make you a pretty poor bet in the marriage stakes.'

Rupert smiled down at her lazily. 'Oh, hopeless odds. No betting woman would take me.'

Sefton refused to be diverted from his own preoccupation. 'You're right. Better never to marry at all. Don't you agree, Cress?'

Startled, Cressida took a quick sip of wine. In trying to change the subject she had never considered the possibility that Sefton in his drunken state might start probing her personal affairs.

'I'm not really qualified to give an opinion,' she began uncomfortably.

He interrupted. 'If you're not, who is? I'm married still. Lord Dearham isn't married at all. You're married *and* divorced. That qualifies you.'

Her eyes flashed and for a moment she felt her temper flare. But one look down the table at Jemima's miserable, flushed face was enough to set a curb on the biting retort she had been about to deliver.

She said carefully, 'When I was getting married, I thought it was the best institution on earth. When I was getting divorced, I was not so happy. Does that answer your question?'

It was not what he was expecting. His blurred eyes stared at her as he frowned, plainly puzzled. Jemima threw her a look of gratitude while Lesley rushed into speech.

'The coffee is bubbling. Do you want to have it here, Cress, or shall I bring it through into the drawing-room? Lucien has left the tray all set out.'

Cressida rose thankfully, opting for the drawing-room, and almost at once Jemima said they should be going. Cressida took her along to her own bedroom to collect her coat from the cupboard.

'I'm sorry about tonight, Cress,' Jemima said. 'Things—aren't easy at the moment.'

Cressida touched her arm. 'Forget it. Everyone has their problems some time.'

'Yes. I'd forgotten.' Jemima hesitated in front of the dressing-table, staring at her reflection with blind eyes. 'Do you still—see him?'

Cressida did not pretend to misunderstand. 'My ex-husband, you mean? Sometimes, yes. He still works for my Papa in the States.'

'Does it hurt? I mean, can you forgive him?'

Cressida shifted uncomfortably. These were questions she did not ask herself. And Jemima Quinn was no close friend of years' standing. Even if she had known the answer she would not have wanted to confide in her. She did not want to confide in anyone.

'It doesn't arise. I don't see him that often. And it's all a long time ago now.'

'Is it? How long?'

That at least was easy. It was a matter of fact and it was an answer she knew. 'Six years.'

'You can't have been married long,' Jemima commented.

Cressida felt her mouth compress into a thin line. Long enough, she could have said. Long enough to learn to despise myself and fear the future.

'Not long, no,' she said in a colourless voice.

'Sefton and I have been married for seventeen years,' Jemima said. 'Surely that makes a difference?'

Her voice was almost pleading but it was not, of course, Cressida to whom she was talking.

'I'm sure it makes a difference,' Cressida said gently, shaking off her own bad memories.

Jemima suddenly lifted her head as if she had been recalled to the present.

'You're a kind girl, Cress,' she said. 'I hope things have worked out for you.'

'I survive,' Cressida told her with a smile.

'And of course your career must take up most of your time and energy. Sefton says you're very successful.' Jemima sounded wistful.

'It depends what you mean by success. I'm good at my job and I enjoy doing it but I sometimes wonder whether I've taken the easy option,' Cressida said honestly.

Jemima slipped her coat round her shoulders. She looked at Cressida curiously.

'Easy? It sounds pretty full-time to me. I'm sure I couldn't handle it.'

'You could if you'd been brought up to it.' Cressida was wry. 'I had my future mapped out for me before I was in secondary school.'

She sounded almost bitter. Jemima Quinn, in spite of her own troubles, was surprised into sympathy.

'Was it not what you wanted? Would you rather do something else?'

But Cressida had finished her uncharacteristic confidences. 'Who knows? I guess we all feel dissatisfied sometimes. We think of the things we might have done, that we haven't done, and get restless.'

Jemima moved to the door, pulling on her gloves. 'There can't be much that you haven't done that you've wanted to do, Cress. Where I've been a good wife and mother so long, I've forgotten whatever it was that I used to want to be.' She squared her shoulders. 'Though if Sefton has his way, I shall have to remember pretty fast. There isn't much of a market for the services of discarded housewives.' She turned in the doorway, saying hesitantly, 'Of course, I know you must be terribly busy, but would you—that is do you think we might get together for tea or a drink or something? I sometimes feel as if all the people I see are on Sefton's side.'

'Surely,' said Cressida, trying to disguise the sinking feeling that invaded her. She liked Jemima and sympathised with her plight but she did not want to be drawn into the Quinns' domestic battles. Still less did she want to be probed about her own private life. And Jemima, it was pathetically clear, wanted to exchange secrets. Cressida had been protecting herself from prying questions for too long to be able to drop her guard now, and she knew it. But now was hardly the time to say so to Jemima Quinn. 'Next week? Tea isn't too easy to fit into my working day but what about an early evening drink? You could come round here again if that is convenient.'

Jemima nodded gratefully. 'I would like that.'

'I haven't got my diary with me, I'm afraid. Anyway, everything is a bit messed up since I cut short my stay in the States. But I'll give you a call tomorrow when I have sorted myself out.'

'Thank you,' Jemima said quietly. 'I appreciate that.'

Cressida gave her a swift, fugitive smile. 'The proverbial drink after work. I don't why housewives aren't as entitled to it as businessmen. I shall look forward to it.'

The Quinns did not leave alone. Selina Forest, looking tired, said that she wanted a reasonably early night. Michael looked slightly annoyed but did not demur, contenting himself with telling Cressida that he would see her in her office the following morning and that she must keep the first hour free for him. Cressida nodded agreement.

'And I'll log it in,' Lesley told Michael Forest on a laugh that turned into an ill-disguised yawn. 'Then she won't be able to get out of it.'

Geoff Singer exchanged a quick silent look with his employer and stood up as well.

'I can see that you're the keeper of Mrs Harley's conscience as well as her diary,' he said pleasantly. 'A responsible job! Do you, too, perhaps, need an early night? May I give you a lift anywhere?'

Lesley was startled and, caught off balance, had no ready reply. She looked at Cressida uncertainly. It was true that she was very weary but nevertheless she did not want to leave her employer alone with Lord Dearham if Cressida wanted her to stay. In general Cressida was good at stage managing departures so that she was never left alone in the apartment at the end of the evening with an unattached male guest who might have ambitions she did not share for ending the entertainment. Tonight was unusual in that Cressida had not shown her usual foresight. Lesley was bewildered. Was it accident that would leave her alone with Rupert Dearham or was it design? And if the latter, was it Rupert's design or Cressida's? In spite of the way she had spoken about him in the car, Lesley had a small suspicion that Cressida was not quite as immune to Lord Dearham's well-publicised charm as she would like to think.

Hesitating, Lesley said, 'Do you need a hand, Cressida? I'm quite happy to help you to clear up, you know.'

Rupert Dearham said smoothly, 'I couldn't permit that, Miss Button. Not when you have so obviously worked hard at preparing this delightful evening. No, no, let Geoff drive you home and I will assist Mrs Harley.'

Cressida's smile was steady. 'You're both very kind but no thank you. I don't intend to do a thing tonight. Lucien and Marthe will deal with it all tomorrow.'

So, thought Lesley, it was not Cressida's idea that Rupert should linger. She bit her lip, not sure what she should do.

'Where is your coat?' asked Geoff Singer, cheerfully impervious.

'In Cressida's cupboard,' Lesley admitted.

'I'll get it,' said Cressida. 'Lord Dearham is right, Lesley. You've done more than enough running around after me today.'

Lesley followed her down the grey-carpeted hall.

'Are you sure?' she asked in a low voice.

Cressida gave her an ironic look over her shoulder as she rummaged in the wardrobe for Lesley's coat. 'Sure that I can fight off Rupert Dearham?' she asked.

Lesley's worried frown deepened. 'Do you think you'll have to?'

'I haven't the slightest idea.' Cressida did not sound worried. 'Like you, I noticed the manoeuvres that were going on. I suppose they had agreed it between them beforehand.'

'Cress, if you're in the slightest bit bothered, I'll stay,' Lesley said earnestly.

The fugitive smile, which revealed an unexpected dimple at the corner of Cressida's mouth, appeared.

'That's true friendship. I can see that you're out on your feet. But it's not necessary. I expect he wants to talk business and I shall shut him up and send him home.'

Lesley was not reassured by this blithe speech.

'What if it isn't just business?'

Cressida's smile became markedly more cynical. 'It's bound to be business, even if it takes the form you obviously think it will. But seriously, it doesn't seem probable.' She cast a passing disparaging look at herself in the full-length mirror on the back of the wardrobe door. 'After all, Lord Dearham is a connoisseur, and what man in his right mind would make a pass at a jet-lagged tycooness who isn't interested?'

Lesley still looked troubled. 'He's very charming.'

'And I'm very tired,' Cressida said firmly. 'Good God, the man's supposed to be an expert. He'll be getting all the signals.'

Lesley allowed herself to be convinced; though she did not miss the look of satisfaction that passed between Geoff Singer and his employer as Geoff was guiding her gently into the lift. She did not like it. She almost turned round and told Cressida that she had changed her mind. But it was too difficult. The lift was there, Geoff had his car keys in his hand, they had said their goodbyes.

Neverthless it was with considerable misgiving that she watched Lord Dearham place a hand under Cressida's elbow and draw her gently back into the hallway of the apartment. As the lift doors closed, Lesley saw Rupert Dearham push the front door of the flat firmly shut and the hall light was snapped off.

In the flat Cressida too was surprised at the proprietorial action. Her head tilted back and her eyes narrowed as she studied the impassive charming mask that was his face.

'Conserving my electricity?' she asked sweetly.

Rupert looked amused. 'You could put it like that.'

This is it, she thought, bracing herself. This is where he reaches for me.

But he did not. He did not move at all.

Cressida swallowed nervously. She was disconcerted. She had not misled Lesley when she said she thought she had nothing to fear from Rupert Dearham. Her opinion of her own attractions was not high, whereas Rupert was not only devastatingly attractive but also obviously used to the highest standards.

Yet there was something in the atmosphere which made her wonder whether she had been wrong; whether Lord Dearham, for whatever private reason of his own, did after all intend to lay hands on her. It did not make sense. But as she stood there in the hallway in the dim light that percolated from the drawing-room, Cressida began to feel alarmed.

It was a feeling with which she was familiar, though she had not had it for a long time. Not for more than six years. She had almost forgotten it. But when he closed the door in that way, moving so that he stood with his back to it as if he were barring her escape, the suppressed memories came rushing back. They burned in her throat.

She took a step back. Never again. It was never going to happen to her again. She could not bear it again.

She said in a deceptively cool voice, 'Can I offer you a final drink? She paused and then added deliberately, 'Before you go.'

Rupert Dearham gave a soft laugh. 'A bribe to get me off the premises? Yes, you can give me a drink, Mrs Harley.'

Cressida did not rise to the challenge she heard in the smooth voice. She led the way back into the lighted room. The gas fire in its huge central chimney was flickering. The standard lamp cast a soft glow over the corner sofa where Rupert Dearham had left his brandy glass. She bent to retrieve it at the same time as he did. Their fingers met on the glass. She let it go at once.

'You're very jumpy,' he said thoughtfully, straightening.

'Jet-lag,' Cressida assured him mendaciously.

'No, it's not jet-lag,' he said with great calm. He poured a dash of cognac into his glass and swirled it. Looking up, he smiled at her across the top of it. 'And don't tell me it's the effect of alcohol either, because I've seen exactly how much you've drunk tonight and you wouldn't get a mouse tight on it.'

Cressida felt her stomach muscles tighten painfully. That smile was so warm, so inviting. Her every instinct was to respond; to smile back, to sink to the sofa where he could join her and they could talk while he smiled into her eyes until ... She caught her careering thoughts. Had she not herself said to Lesley that this man was dangerous? Now he was proving it with that deceptive charm.

She moved away and perched on the arm of a sleek Danish chair. The pose looked, she hoped, suitably impermanent, a silent reminder that he was soon to leave. Rupert flung himself down on the sofa, still watching her, and stretched a languid arm along the back of its cushions. He was smiling. For no reason that she could think of, Cressida put up both hands to the lapels of her blouse and drew it closed, though it had hardly been revealing before. Rupert's smile widened. She looked at him with dislike.

'I am not,' she said with precision, 'jumpy. Or tight. Or, for that matter, a mouse.'

'No?' It was asked very softly.

'No.'

He raised the brandy glass to his lips for a moment. Then, not looking at her, 'Prove it?' he invited.

Recognising danger, Cressida went very still. The sea-green eyes lifted and fastened on her mouth. She shuddered as if he had touched her, though he made no other movement.

'How?' she said through stiff lips. It was meant to be scornful but, even to her own ears she sounded plain scared.

Rupert looked at her consideringly. She was not sure if there were some long-term strategy involved or whether it was sheer devilry of the moment but she was not surprised when he murmured, 'Kiss me goodnight and I'll go.'

Her mouth was dry. In spite of the Scandinavian hearth and the background heating, she was very cold. Under the brilliant taffeta of her blouse, her skin was shivering. She could not bear it. She *could* not.

Cressida said icily, 'I would prefer it if you left unkissed.'

'How unkind,' he mourned, his eyes gleaming. 'So beautiful and yet so cruel!' He heaved a theatrical sigh.

Cressida was aware that she was being teased and strove for a lighter tone.

'Neither the one, nor the other, Lord Dearham, but very tired, so if you will excuse me ...'

But he interrupted, ignoring the rider. 'Oh yes,' he

said very seriously. 'You're beautiful. Haven't they told you that?'

Suddenly she was angry. What right had he to tease her like this? She knew how plain she was, how lacking in fire and mystery and all the things that, according to Keith Harley, were essential in an attractive woman. She stood up.

'Don't let us play games, Lord Dearham,' she said crisply. 'What do you want?'

He tipped his head back to stare into her face. His eyes narrowed.

'I think I just told you,' he pointed out.

Cressida dismissed it. 'Nonsense.'

'Is it?'

'Lord Dearham,' she said with ostentatious restraint, 'you and I have met twice and on neither occasion have you impressed me as a fool. So if you are sitting around in my drawing-room making yourself obnoxious when it is quite clear that I would rather you went home, it must be because you want more than the dubious pleasure of a good night kiss from me.'

His eyebrows met in a quick frown.

'Well?' she said challengingly.

The steep lids hooded his eyes; the long mouth curled into a smile.

'You're right, of course,' sighed Rupert Dearham, getting composedly to his feet. 'I want a lot more than a good night kiss.'

And then he did reach for her. When she was angry and unprepared and vulnerable.

There was nothing violent in the movement. His grip was firm but it did not bruise and his mouth was quite gentle. There was no justification for Cressida's freezing into panting immobility like a desperate, hunted creature.

He felt it, of course. Almost before he had feathered a kiss across her lips, he was holding her a little way

away from him, searching her pale face with a grim
expression. Cressida closed her eyes and turned her
head away. She knew what happened next. Had she not
experienced it a hundred times; and promised herself
that she would free herself from it for ever? And
tonight, stupid and over-confident, she had let Lesley
go off with Geoff Singer leaving her at the mercy of a
man who was clearly as savage a predator as ever Keith
Harley had been.

'What's the matter, *Mrs* Harley?' Rupert said
mockingly. 'Scruples?'

Cressida's throat moved but no sound emerged. He
gave a gentle shake.

'You're not being very scientific about this. Or,' he
added thoughtfully, 'very enthusiastic.'

This time she managed to speak. 'About what?'

The strange eyes gleamed. 'About carrying out your
father's instructions.'

She stared at him dumbfounded.

'To seduce me,' he reminded her softly.

A slow tide of colour washed into her face. 'You
heard,' she said in a small voice.

'I imagine the whole building heard.' His voice was
hard, indifferent.

Cressida lifted her chin. 'Nobody heard me agree,
however.'

'No, but you took the next plane back to be here
tonight, didn't you?'

She was in a trap. She had already made him a present
of the information that she had flown back specially, that
her original plan had been to stay in New York for much
longer. She listened with creeping horror as he went on.

'I must say I was intrigued. Your father is an
original, of course. I haven't met many people who
conduct their business dealings in quite the way he
does. But I didn't expect even Jerome Sebastian to offer
quite such an—er—inducement.'

Humiliation worse than she had ever experienced took hold of her. And she was an expert on humiliation. She had lived with it as a daily companion for months until Keith had finally declared that he wanted a divorce. But even cold and unresponsive under his taunts, she had never felt as shamed as she did now before this man. And shame locked her tongue.

'It is a new experience for me,' Rupert Dearham said reflectively. 'And I cannot resist new experiences.'

His arms tightened. In horror, she brought up her hands flat against his chest, pushing him away. She was weak and her action made no impression on him. But feeling his heart's steady rhythm under the crisp shirt set Cressida trembling.

'Please . . .' It was a thread of a sound. She did not even know what she was pleading for, unless it was understanding. Perhaps a measure of compassion.

It fell on deaf ears. Rupert was laughing. 'Losing your nerve, Cressida Harley?' He shook his head reprovingly. 'What would Daddy say? If you don't like me, sweetheart, close your eyes and pretend I'm the absent Mr Harley. Or whoever it was that you left the poor devil for.'

She said hopelessly, 'Let me go.'

He chuckled. 'With Operation Dearham uncompleted? You don't mean that.'

'Look,' Cressida said, controlling her panic by a thread, 'whatever you believe, as far as I'm concerned Operation Dearham never started.'

The hand he passed over her hair was oddly tender. But he was implacable.

'I might have believed you, my angel, were it not for your efficiency. This evening has run like clockwork. They were all breathless with admiration—the wit, the charm, the glamour . . .'

Cressida felt as if she were caught in a nightmare; only she knew that there would be no welcome waking to hail her out of it, back to the kind and normal world.

'The glamour is just the clothes,' she said desperately. She was beginning to shake in earnest.

It was the wrong thing to say. Rupert smiled down at her.

'Well, we can easily get rid of them,' he told her gently.

She stared up at him, disbelieving. This could not be happening. Not after all these years, after all her care to avoid giving any man the illusion of possessing rights in her or her time. It was simply not possible that because of a few heated words of her father's and her own misplaced confidence, the first time her vigilance failed she would end up wounded and humiliated in a stranger's arms.

Without haste Rupert undid the clasp that held the ruff in place under her chin. It opened and the ruff fell away, leaving her throat bare. For a moment he held her still in his hands, the opaque eyes scanning her. Then, with precision, he bent and set his lips to the exact place at the base of her throat where the pulse was beating frantically.

Cressida made a small sound of distress, standing as if turned to stone. His mouth was warm and infinitely sensual. She had never experienced anything more terrifying in her life.

His hands moved down her body, moulding her against him. She did not resist. To him, it must have seemed as if she were pliant because she was willing, trembling in anticipation. He would think, Cressida realised in blank misery, that this was the easy conquest of a passionate body made hungry by experience. Whereas the reality was so different it was laughable.

Cressida made no attempt to free herself. Experience had not made her hungry but it had taught her that to struggle sometimes had the opposite effect from what was intended. She breathed carefully, trying to think.

Suddenly, so suddenly that she was taken by surprise

and cried out, Rupert swung her off her feet. Behind
her the starched ruff fell to the rug.

He smiled down into her dazed eyes, 'Time for bed, I
think.'

He knew which door led to her room. It was easy
enough for him to find out, of course. It was no secret
and all the women had left their coats there when they
arrived. But the fact that he had bothered to find out
argued both that this incident was planned and that he
had planned many other such incidents in the past.
Cressida found it chilling.

He lowered her on to her bed very gently and began
to kiss her. She was shaking so much she could barely
feel it. He would take that for uncontrollable lust, of
course.

When he raised his head Cressida said earnestly,
'Please don't do this.'

'Not even at parental instigation?' Rupert said
teasingly. 'And everyone told me you were a Daddy's girl.'

He slid his hands inside the taffeta jacket, moulding
her shoulders, caressing the taut length of her collar
bone. Cressida closed her eyes.

The new few minutes were a revelation. He was, she
recognised bitterly, an expert at seduction. She disliked
and feared him but he was still able to caress her flesh
into trembling awareness. She had never known
anything like the sensations evoked by his mouth on her
breast or the deceptively tender touch of his tongue on
the soft inner skin of her elbow. If it hadn't been that
she knew what shaming violence would follow, she
would be melting as he drew the clothes away from her,
turning to him with longing as she had once expected to
turn to Keith.

A long shudder went through her as he kissed her
mouth. His control was going now, his breathing fast
and shallow and the force in the kiss was a hateful echo
of all that she remembered. She shut her eyes tight, no

longer trying to find a way of escape, concentrating instead on how she would endure it.

Rupert gave a long sigh and raised his head. She had been wrong about his control. His breathing was unruffled.

'You know,' he said reflectively, winding an escaped curl round his finger as he looked down at her silent figure, 'I don't think I like the games you play, Cressida Harley.'

She opened her eyes, bewildered. He was very close, of course, and it took her a second to focus. When she did, she realised that he was angry.

'What do you mean?' she whispered.

'I think I must have given you the wrong idea,' he mused. 'When I said I liked new experiences, I meant within reason.' He paused. 'New experiences, yes. Rape, no,' he explained softly, as she continued to stare at him.

He did not sound angry, she thought in confusion. He sounded light and uncaring and utterly sophisticated. But his eyes were molten with fury. She felt scorched by it.

In a sudden movement he leaned over her, trapping her body between his arms, holding her face by the chin so that she could not turn away from that basilisk stare.

'Kiss me,' he demanded, whispering. It was a challenge. She closed her eyes in panic and his fingers tightened. 'Touch me!'

There was absolute silence in the shuttered bedroom. Cressida lay as quiet as a mouse, hardly daring to breathe. It was more like a nightmare than ever. If I don't move, if I don't speak, if I don't blink, perhaps he will let me go, she thought frantically.

And then, amazingly, he did, spinning away from her across the double bed that had been bought for her and Keith and never used by them. Greatly daring, she risked a look at him under her lashes. His face was set, angry, but he was not preparing to launch an attack.

He was doing up the top button of his shirt with vicious movements.

But when he spoke his voice was still that soft, amused drawl. 'Somewhere in all this drama I've lost my tie. You must let me have it back some time.'

He swung off the bed and came round to the side where she lay. For a moment he looked down at her, his face inscrutable.

'You're going to have trouble explaining this to Daddy,' he said at last, with a grin. He reached down and touched his forefinger to her cheek in a gesture so gentle that she almost responded. 'You'll have to tell him you play too rough for me.' The grin widened, the eyes stayed cold. 'I'm sure it won't surprise him.'

He turned and left. Cressida heard the front door shut behind him and then, more dimly, the soft whirr of machinery as he took the lift to the ground floor. She did not move.

CHAPTER THREE

THE morning was a disaster. For one thing Cressida had still not shaken off New York time. For another she had slept badly, racked by vivid and frightening dreams. The two conditions combined to make her oversleep by an unheard-of three hours.

When she emerged from her bedroom, heavy-eyed and yawning, it was to meet Marthe le Puy in the corridor.

'Would you like breakfast in bed, Miss Cress?' she asked in a motherly way. 'You are not going to work this morning, are you?'

Cressida looked at her slim gold wristwatch and groaned.

'Well, I was *supposed* to. But I imagine you're right: I won't make it before midday,' she agreed ruefully.

'I will bring you in a tray,' Marthe announced.

But Cressida shook her head. 'No, honestly, I couldn't eat a thing. I'll just raid the refrigerator for an orange juice and get going.'

Lucien was in the kitchen. He looked up with a smile when she came in.

'A late night, Miss Cressida?'

Cressida nodded. He went to the refrigerator and poured her a tall glass of the freshly squeezed juice that he had prepared that morning. She sipped it gratefully.

'Are there any messages?' she asked, not expecting that there would be. People who wanted to contact her left messages with her office. Or else they wrote to the jealously guarded private address. 'Post?'

'There is a message on the Ansaphone,' Lucien told her. 'Mr Jerome must have tried to contact you last night.'

43

Cressida made a face. 'I forgot to unhook the answering machine when I got in. It will have taken all the calls last night. Blast.'

'I think Mr Jerome rang several times. That would account for it,' Lucien told her, composedly returning washed china to its cupboard.

'Oh dear. That means he'll be furious,' said Cressida with foreboding. 'Again.'

'It is too early in New York to ring him yet,' Lucien said comfortingly.

'True. I'll have to do it this afternoon from the office.' Cressida finished her juice and stood up. 'It's obviously going to be one of those days. I've missed a meeting with Michael Forest which he said was important. And now I've dropped a phone call from my father: and Papa thinks all his messages are important. I wonder what else can go wrong?'

She wandered back to her room. She had her own bathroom off her bedroom. It had been designed by Jerome's Countess presumably to suit her own taste. Cressida always felt faintly uncomfortable in it. It was all white and gold, the bath a sculpted shell, the shower attachment an arching swan's neck in gold. The battered navy robe looked incongruous as she hung it on the golden outstretched hands that served as hooks.

She showered quickly and changed into a business suit. Then she unpacked two of her cases with swift efficiency. Washing went in one pile, toilet things returned to the suitcase for the next outing, books and papers were set aside for taking to the office, and unworn clothes—of which this time there were a fair number—went rapidly back into her wardrobe.

Cressida had nearly finished when there was a soft knock on the door. Expecting Marthe she turned with a smile, but it was not the familiar face but a much younger and prettier one. For a moment Cressida was puzzled. Then she recalled that Marthe had told her she was going to hire a girl from the agency to do some of the cleaning while she, Marthe, recovered from an operation for varicose veins. This, presumably, was the result.

'Good morning,' Cressida said. 'Did you want to clean my room? I'm afraid I seem to have overslept.'

The girl nodded, giving her a shy smile, and went to the bed, pulling back the tumbled bedclothes that told their own tale of Cressida's disturbed night.

'If it is not convenient I can go to another room,' she said carefully in accented English.

'No, I'm on my way,' Cressida assured her, snapping the wardrobe door shut and picking up an armful of papers.

The girl bobbed her head and began to straighten the bed. Then she bent suddenly. As Cressida turned from one last check through of her paperwork, the girl stood up looking puzzled. From her fingers dangled a slightly crushed but unmistakable undone bow tie.

Cressida stopped dead. It had obviously fallen among the bed covers. Rupert had said he had lost it. She distinctly remembered that he had said he had lost it. And now here it was, bearing silent but incontrovertible witness that he had been here on her bed last night.

Having tried to put the incident out of her mind ever since she woke up, Cressida felt slightly sick at being reminded so forcibly of it. She put out a reluctant hand to take it from the girl. She did not want to touch it.

But it was not possible to say that. So she thrust it into the pocket of her jacket and said, 'Thank you,' without expression.

The girl avoided her eyes. She seemed embarrassed. Which makes two of us, thought Cressida sourly. Damn Rupert Dearham.

She went into the drawing-room. Before she left she had better listen to her father's messages. He would expect her to be up to date on whatever it was that he wanted to talk to her about when she called him back.

Marthe was there, dusting out the now dead hearth. She looked up at Cressida's approach.

'I rang Miss Button and told her you would be late. She's sending the car for you.'

'There was no need,' said Cressida, as always slightly shocked by the care that her staff lavished on her. 'I could perfectly well have taken the underground.'

'It gets pretty crowded at lunchtime. Miss Button is right,' said Marthe.

Cressida went to the answering machine and played back the tape. To her surprise, her father sounded anxious rather than angry. Presumably he was suffering pangs of conscience about the things he had shouted at her, thought Cressida wryly. He would want to make up, assure her of his love and concern—and be reassured in his turn. She sighed. He was like a child. He thought he only had to say he was sorry and that wiped out all the hurt and insult he had delivered when he was in a temper. One day he would find he was wrong and, Cressida was pretty sure, he would be devastated. He had nearly driven her to the brink this time. On the plane home she had been seriously considering resignation.

'Mr Jerome all right?' asked Marthe, who knew about his heart condition.

Cressida smiled. 'Fighting fit when I last saw him. And just a bit ashamed of himself now, to judge by the messages.'

Marthe, a long-standing family confidante, nodded her head in understanding.

'You're too good to him, Miss Cress. He don't know when he's lucky.'

'I doubt if Papa would agree with you.' Cressida stood up, stretching. 'He wouldn't approve of the hours I'm keeping this morning, for example.'

Marthe gave her a huge smile. 'Every girl needs to lie in late once in a while,' she said, adding with apparent inconsequentiality, 'you have a good time with that Lord Dearham last night? My, now there's a handsome man.'

Cressida's eyes narrowed. 'Lord Dearham was not my only guest, Marthe.'

Marthe was undisturbed. 'No, but he was the one it was all for, wasn't he, honey? You like him a lot?'

Cressida did not answer that directly. 'What are you suggesting, Marthe?' she asked slowly.

'You don't have to lie to me, honey,' the housekeeper said in a comfortable voice. 'I won't go telling your Papa, nor yet the newspapers.'

And she offered, for Cressida's inspection, the starched ruff of last night's outfit, now neatly folded.

'It was on the rug,' Marthe said matter-of-factly, 'by the sofa. And when I looked in on you this morning, you were sleeping like a babe with all your clothes in a heap by the bed. I picked them up for you. Didn't you notice?'

'Oh, God,' said Cressida with feeling.

'Now don't you start to fuss, Miss Cress. You ain't done nothing to be ashamed of. Nor it ain't nobody's business but yours.' Marthe's satisfied grin belied this last statement. She was savouring Cressida's supposed night of love with generous enthusiasm. 'And it ain't before time, either.'

The bell which summoned the penthouse lift rang. Marthe marched over to the control panel and picked up the receiver, listening.

'It's the car,' she told Cress. 'You going down now?'

'I—no—that is, yes, I suppose so,' said Cressida distractedly. 'Look, Marthe, it isn't what you think between Lord Dearham and me. Honestly.'

Marthe patted her arm. 'Don't matter to me, one way or the other. You enjoy yourself, honey,' she said, clearly unconvinced.

'I—oh, well, I've got to go. I'll see you later.' And

Cressida fled from Marthe's congratulatory smile, feeling hunted.

Well, she had wondered what else could go wrong and now she had found out. First the girl from the agency—who would presumably tell Marthe and Lucien of her discovery—and then Marthe, both of them obviously assured that she had kicked over the traces in no uncertain terms and, totally out of character, done it in the company of Rupert Dearham.

Cresside settled back in the Rolls' luxurious upholstery and tried to be philosophical. What did it matter, after all? Why was she so upset that anyone should think she was having an affair with Lord Dearham? As Marthe said, it was nobody's business but her own whether she was or was not. Even if it got into the papers, she did not care. She had grown adept at avoiding reporters over the years and she did not think they had much interest in her these days. And if her father found out, well—she shrugged—she would say he had only himself to blame. It was what he had told her to do, after all. He would be hoist with his own petard and it was, if anything, rather funny.

Yet she could not shake off that feeling of distate. It was silly, she knew. Perhaps it stemmed from the fact that, for a couple of seconds last night, she had almost found herself imagining what it would be like to be Rupert Dearham's lover. Now that was *really* out of character, much more than this foolish reaction to Marthe's suspicions.

But if only Marthe had not been so delighted, Cressida thought. That had hurt, too. And she had no idea at all why it should be so.

She was frowning when the Rolls drew up outside the porticoes of Sebastian House in the City. The chief messenger came forward to open the door, take her substantial briefcase and help her out. He was very correct, as always, but the smile he gave her was warm.

I am surrounded by people who have known me from my cradle and wish me nothing but good, thought Cressida with wry self-mockery. I wonder if Sam would be as delighted as Marthe if he thought I'd spent the night with Rupert Dearham? Probably he would.

It was oddly depressing, as if it pointed to a lack in her present life which her wellwishers had identified and she had not. She shook off the depression, giving him her usual shy smile and a word of thanks before she dived into the lift that took her into her office.

At an enormous mahogany desk in a window that overlooked London, Lesley Button surveyed her employer's hurried entrance with some amusement.

'Oversleep?'

'And how,' agreed Cressida. 'Hours!'

'When the Sebastians do things, they do them in a big way,' agreed Lesley. 'I sent Michael Forest back to his padded cell but he's left a file that he says you must look at before you sign anything with Lord Dearham.'

'Oh?' Cressida managed not to blush at the name but she could not help a tinge of self-consciousness in the tone. 'Does he think Lord Dearham's company is trying to rook us?'

Lesley shook her head. 'He did not say. But he's definitely not in favour of the acquisition. I imagine'— she looked down at her blotter and chose her words carefully, 'that he wants you to tell Mr Jerome so.'

'It being a pet project of Papa's?' murmured Cressida. 'I see. Has he tried telling Papa himself, do you know?'

Lesley hesitated. 'Well—I think that Michael was asked to prepare a report on the company in the first place. Before anyone knew that Mr Sebastian thought of buying it. Michael was quite keen on it as a business partner.'

'But he doesn't want it as a subsidiary?' Cressida nodded. 'All right, I'll read his report and if it makes

sense I'll give Papa the bad news that his finance
director thinks he's making a mistake.' She gave her
attractive low chuckle. 'That'll make the second time he
fires me this week.'

Relieved, Lesley pushed a slim folder across the desk.

'Is this all?' asked Cressida surprised, used to Michael
Forest's voluminous presentations.

'He says you've got all the background papers.'

'I suppose I must have. They were what I took to
New York. Call them up for me, will you, Lesley? I'll
go over it this afternoon.'

Cressida went into her private office, leaving the door
ajar.

'Oh, and get me New York as early as possible.
Papa was trying to reach me last night.'

She went through the papers for her attention with
practised speed. Apart from Michael's report nothing
needed close attention. She signed three letters which
she had dictated before she left for the States, approved
a promotion which was already agreed and made a
recommendation on three candidates for a new job who
had been referred to her from the personnel department.
Most of her incoming mail would be dealt with by
subordinates and she made a note to Lesley about who
should be delegated to answer various queries.

Cressida worked steadily for a couple of hours before
Lesley buzzed her.

'Your call to Mr Sebastian.'

'Thanks,' said Cressida, picking up the telephone
warily. 'Hello, Papa. My answering machine tells me
you've been chasing me.'

'Damned thing,' he grumbled but he sounded subdued.

'What is it?'

'It's sort of personal.' Jerome Sebastian was
unwontedly hesitant.

'Papa, when are you ever anything else?' teased
Cressida.

'No, this is different.' He paused and a few seconds of expensive silence ticked away before he blurted out, 'Cress, Keith has been to see me.'

'Yes?' She was puzzled but unmoved. Keith Harley worked for Jerome on the American west coast and was one of his most highly trusted and respected deputies. They met frequently.

'He's very unhappy.'

Cressida's mouth tightened. Keith Harley was a favourite of her father's. She had been more or less thrust into his arms and her father had never forgiven her for the break-up of the marriage he had engineered.

'So raise his salary,' she said flippantly.

'Don't talk like that, Cress. You sound so hard. It isn't like you.'

'No? I think I became pretty hard about Keith's feelings some years ago. As I recall it was mutual.'

'What do you mean?' demanded Jerome. He sounded peevish.

'I mean that Keith didn't give a damn about me then and doesn't now. And it is reciprocated,' Cressida told him coolly.

'Now that's where you're wrong. He cares a lot about you. That's why he's so unhappy. He tells me you've refused to see him.'

Cressida stared at the telephone in disbelief. 'Papa, are you serious?'

'He's no longer with that girl,' Jerome said in a wheedling tone, prudently ignoring her question. 'He misses you. He told me he knew he made a mistake when he left you. Of course, you were both very young and I don't for a moment think he was the only one to blame . . .' He was on firmer ground now and his tone became hectoring. 'You were silly and immature and you had no idea about men. But you're older now, both of you, and you'll have learned something.'

'Yes, Papa,' Cressida interrupted. 'I've learned to

steer clear of men like Keith Harley. I don't know what sentimental rubbish you've been telling each other but I don't for a moment believe that Keith is yearning to return to me. And if I did, I'd be sorry because so far as I'm concerned it's too late. You would be doing him no kindness and making yourself look a great fool if you led him to believe anything else.'

There was, predictably, an explosion. Cressida put the telephone on the vertical cradle that held it when she was putting a caller on room-wide amplification. She made no attempt to answer him. There was no point in trying to interrupt Jerome Sebastian in full flow. She signed off a routine report on monthly liquidity and put it in the out tray.

Eventually even Jerome ran out of breath.

'He's coming over to England. I'm sending him over on business. You're to see him and that's an order.'

'I'll see him on business, sure,' agreed Cressida.

Her father gave a baffled roar. 'You'll do as you're told. He wants to spend some time with you.'

'Papa,' said Cressida quietly. 'You do not own me. You employ me. And that could be changed.'

She shut off his fury with a quick flick of the wrist, breaking the connection. Then she buzzed Lesley.

'Today is cancelled,' she told her secretary grimly. 'I have a feeling it was a mistake getting out of bed. I am going to take Michael Forest's report and I am going home. You are not to tell anyone where I have gone, particularly not my father.'

'Right,' said Lesley, unperturbed. 'Your diary is clear because you were supposed to be in New York, so you can stay through till next week if you want.'

'I might just do that,' said Cressida. She hesitated, thinking of the threatened visit of her ex-husband. For a moment she was tempted to tell Lesley, to ask her to warn her at the cottage if Keith arrived at Sebastian House.

She rejected the idea. As far as the Sebastian employees were concerned, the Harley marriage had been a mistake which had ended amicably with reasonable good will on both sides. It was the only possible story if Keith were to keep his position in the company, albeit out of England, and Cressida were to retain some measure of dignity. She was not going to undermine that story now, by the slightest hint, even to someone she trusted as much as she trusted Lesley. After all she trusted Marthe and Lucien and they did not know the truth of her miserable marriage, either.

Cressida rang the basement car park and asked the head chauffeur to have her own car ready. It was a new, low cabriolet, fast and silent. Her car was virtually Cressida's only personal extravagance.

On her way out she stopped by Lesley's desk as a thought struck her,

'I'd better ring Marthe. I unpacked in a hurry and left a pile of washing on the bedroom floor. If I don't tell her not, she'll wash it for me.'

'Some people,' said Lesley, dialling the number of the flat, 'don't know when they're well off.' She handed the receiver to her employer with a grin. 'Oh, for someone to do *my* washing!'

'Marthe has quite enough to do as the housekeeper. She's not paid to clear up after me,' said Cressida. Then the housekeeper came on the line and she spoke to her briefly, explaining that she would be in her retreat and was not in any circumstances to be disturbed, while the washing was to go in the laundry basket.

When she put the telephone down Lesley said slowly, 'You ought to have a maid. Anyone else in your position would.'

Cressida made a face. 'I have little enough privacy as it is without surrendering more to a lady's maid. Compared with that, doing my own washing is a small price to pay.'

'If you say so,' said Lesley, unconvinced. She looked down at her notebook. 'What do I tell your father when he calls?'

'I've taken a few days' holiday, you don't know where.'

'Right. And do you want me to ring you at all? Keep you up to date?'

'Yes, I suppose you'd better,' Cressida agreed without enthusiasm. 'Though I have this feeling I'd like to cut myself off completely for a while. Feel free. Do you know what I mean?'

'Yes,' said Lesley gently. 'Yes, I know what you mean. And I won't interrupt unless it's urgent. Have a good break.'

Cressida smiled an acknowledgment and ran lightly down the spiral staircase to the garage. It was cool in the basement but she knew well that outside the temperature was in the eighties and the sunlight was as dazzling as it could be in London. She got her keys from the chauffeur, who had backed her car out of its stall and had it ready for her on the slipway. Then, tossing Michael's report on the passenger seat and stowing her briefcase under it, she swung her long legs into the car, wound down the window and drove off with a wave at the chauffeurs' cabin.

It was a good drive out of London, between rush hours. The motorway was nearly empty. The car drifted along it like a bird. The top was down and Cressida savoured the warm breeze that lifted her hair. For the first time for weeks she began to relax.

She came in sight of the cottage by late afternoon. It was down a rutted track that the Mercedes took like a lady. The track led nowhere else, just to the small thatched cottage set in its gardens and orchard with the stream curling round it. The front garden was hedged by a high trellis covered in honeysuckle, but above this towered hollyhocks in profusion and tall delphiniums.

Cressida coasted the car to a halt, switched off the engine and sat back, looking at her domain with a sigh of absolute pleasure. This was her secret place, her home. This was where she was the person that, underneath successful Cressida Harley, she felt she really was. This was where she was at peace.

There was no garage attached to the cottage. From time to time Cressida thought of building one and then forgot about it. It hardly seemed important. She left the Mercedes in the lee of the hedge, pulled well off the track in case the farmer wanted to bring his tractor down the lane as he did twice a year. Then she let herself into the house.

It was very warm and still, smelling of rose leaves and woodsmoke. She had left everything tidy before she went, so there were no piles of old magazines or rumpled rugs to offend the eye. But there was a fine film of dust on all the surfaces of the wooden furniture that she loved to keep highly polished. The brass and copper had lost their sheen. And the vases were empty.

Cressida went to the low leaded window that overlooked the garden from the hallway. There was a Stuart oak chest in front of it on which she kept a copper jug, always full of flowers while she was in residence. She knelt on the chest to open the window. It was a little stiff but she managed to dislodge it at last and the scents of the garden rushed in upon her: verbena and wallflowers, pinks and roses. Her nose twitched in pleasure.

She went through the small house opening the windows wide, displacing ornaments and tumbling curtains until it looked lived in and homelike again. Then, and only then, she changed into shorts and a light muslin top and went out into her garden.

She sat on the flat stone above the stream, looking down into the water. There were weeds between the paving stones, she noted, a fine crop of groundsel in the rosebed and the beginning of stinging nettles between the lavender and rosemary. She would have a fine day's weeding tomorrow. The lawn needed cutting, too. She liked mowing the lawn with her ancient machine. It took ages and was very soothing.

Lost in a pleasurable reverie of anticipation, she was startled to hear herself hailed. She looked round to find her neighbour coming towards her down the stream track, bearing a bottle of milk. Smiling, she waved to him.

'Wife said you were back,' Vic told her placidly. 'Dogs heard the car. Seen the cats yet?'

When Cressida first bought the cottage it had been all but derelict and given over to mice. She had acquired two cats who, having seen off the rodents, settled down to a peaceful existence of sleeping on spare beds and catching fish from the stream. When she was away Vic and his wife Rose fed the cats but they still lived in the cottage, letting themselves in and out through the catflap. On a baking hot afternoon the cats would, Cressida was well aware, be stretched out somewhere in the orchard snoozing blissfully.

'No. Have they behaved?'

'Two pigeons, one stickleback, a couple of mice and a goldfish,' reported Vic. 'All laid out on the step, same as usual. They're good hunters, them cats.'

'Ugh!' Cressida gave an exaggerated shiver. 'I'm sorry you had to clear their booty away.'

He grinned. 'It's their nature, you can't blame them. And they're pleased as punch with themselves when they've caught something.'

'I just hope they don't bring me any little offerings tonight,' said Cressida gloomily as he prepared to move off up the stream, his dog at his heels.

''Tis a compliment,' he said, disappearing with a wave.

She leaned back on her stone, tipping her face up to

the sun. Oh, it felt so good to be here. The neighbours were kind and blessedly incurious. The estate agent she had employed to buy the house had misheard her name and always called her Miss Bastion. So Miss Bastion she had become for the village. They knew she was well off, because of the car, but they had no idea what she did or who she really was. They were not interested.

There had at first been a flurry of curiosity about the maiden lady buying Blackbird Cottage. When she turned out to be young and attractive there were dark predictions that she would be holding orgies full of wicked Londoners. As, however, neither the orgies nor hordes of urban guests appeared and Miss Bastion seemed very contented tending her garden and reading the unhealthy number of books that filled the cottage, the village had lost interest. It was, in their unexpressed opinion, pretty disappointing.

Cressida herself was quite aware that she had not come up to their expectations. It had been made plain to her from the vicar's all-too-obvious relief to the post office lady's equally obvious regret.

She smiled now, thinking of it as she stretched in the sun. Little did they know how unlikely she was to allow sophistication to invade her domain here. Bill and Dandy Cartwright, cottage dwellers themselves, had been to stay a couple of times. So had old Dicky Hubert who used to drive her father before he retired and had insisted on presenting her with a tray of his own geranium seedlings. Lesley knew where it was and had been to dinner. Jerome Sebastian had neither the address nor the telephone number. And Keith Harley did not even know it existed.

Cressida felt warm and safe and languorous as she turned over on her stomach and saw the junior cat make its leisurely way towards her through the long grass and buttercups. She dropped her chin to her laced fingers and finally drifted off to sleep.

When she woke it was to the distinct impression of being delicately pushed. It must be a cat, she decided drowsily, and put a hand down to repel her furry assailant. Her hand was caught and held in a firm clasp.

Instantly she was awake, jack-knifing out of sleep like a diver off a high board. She swung round and up into a sitting position, her eyes wide and alarmed, and came face to face with the lazy amusement of Lord Dearham.

'*You!*'

'As you say.' He hunkered down beside her, so that his face was on a level with her own. The sea-green eyes were very bright. 'As you see.'

Cressida was shaken. She was breathless with shock.

'What are you doing here?'

'For that matter, what are you?' he countered. 'Running away?'

'No, of course not,' said Cressida, outraged. 'This is my home.'

Something flickered in his eyes. 'Really?'

'Yes, really,' she retorted with heat. 'And I want to know what you're doing in it.'

'Ah. Yes.' He looked down at her long tanned legs. 'Well, you see, I rather thought I owed you an apology. After last night, you see.'

Cressida stared at him, uncomprehending. He gave a little laugh.

'Don't look so amazed. I can admit when I'm in the wrong as much as the next man. And on reflection I have decided that last night I was about as wrong as I could be. Wasn't I?'

She did not answer that. She said slowly, 'You have driven all the way down here just to say you're *sorry*?'

The mobile mouth twisted. 'Don't the men in your life usually say they're sorry when they've hurt you, Cressida Harley?'

She shook her head, dazed. The loosened auburn hair

fell about her neck. Rupert Dearham watched it as if fascinated.

'I don't understand.'

'And yet it's very simple. I left with a bad taste in my mouth last night. You looked so white. Terrified, almost. I rang this morning but the admirable Miss Button said you were not yet in, though she was expecting you. I thought you'd probably had a bad night and it was down to me.'

He gave a quick look at her bemused face but she said nothing. After a pause he went on, 'Then I went to Sebastian House this afternoon. You'd gone, weren't to be disturbed.'

'Are you saying Lesley gave you this address?' Cressida could hardly believe it, not after her express instructions.

'No. By no means. She was very discreet and rather disapproving. It was a charming large black lady with a French accent who told me where to find you. Unlike your secretary,' Rupert added reflectively, 'she seemed to wish me well.'

'Marthe's a romantic,' said Cressida curtly. Damn, damn, *damn* that sentimentality. Marthe had had him marked out and on stage as Cressida's new lover, even before he turned up at the flat asking for her. Why had it not occurred to her to forbid Lucien and Marthe to give her address to anyone?

Because, said a small voice, they would never normally have done it. Because they have never done it before. It is only Rupert Dearham for whom they would breach their normal discreet silence.

'Is she?' Rupert sounded amused. 'She struck me as decidedly down to earth.'

Cressida flicked him a look of dislike. She knew exactly what he meant. Marthe would have left him in little doubt of what she imagined was his relationship with Cressida and her whole-hearted approval of it.

Cressida could only hope that she had not regaled him with tales of Cressida from the age of eight, an activity towards which she inclined.

'So you've come to apologise.' Her voice was flat. 'You've apologised. Thank you. Goodbye.'

Rupert did not move. 'Not just to apologise.' His voice was very soft.

Cressida looked at him warily. 'What then?'

He weighed his words, seeming to choose them with care. 'To find out why I was so wrong. To reassure you. To know what you're running away from.' He smiled. 'And to do a little chemical research.'

She was completely taken aback. For a wild moment she thought he was referring to some project in the countryside and looked rapidly round her well-stocked garden.

'Chemical research?'

'Yes,' said Rupert Dearham, trapping her face between his hands and bending towards her. 'Body chemistry.'

CHAPTER FOUR

IT was not, in spite of his avowed intentions, a reassuring speech. Still less was it a reassuring kiss. Before Cressida knew what he was doing, Rupert had sought and found her mouth in a slow exploration that caused a trembling to start deep in the centre of her body.

He moved subtly, settling her against his chest so that she could not move in any direction except closer to him. His hands on her sunwarmed back felt like iron. Through unfocused eyes she watched the light fracture into a hundred rainbows from his long downswept lashes. He looked intent, serious, and the long sensuous kiss felt serious too.

With a little moan, Cressida shut her eyes, giving herself up for a moment to unexpected sensations. She felt she was being teased, coaxed down that untrodden path that she feared so greatly. Yet at the same time she was not afraid. The persuasive lips were luring her into response but there was no force, no threat in the delicate mastery.

At last, slowly, he raised his head, letting her draw a little away from him yet not letting her go completely.

'There,' he said softly, as if he had propounded a point and proved it.

Shaken, Cressida put up the back of her right hand to her lips.

'Did you have to do that?' she said in a small voice.

Rupert smiled down at her through narrowed lids. 'Yes, I think so.'

She made a despairing gesture. 'What does it prove?'

He took her hand from her lips, turned it over and

looked down at the taut knuckles with an odd smile.
'Perhaps that I can want a woman without being a
brute about it?' he offered. He raised her hand to his
mouth and brushed his lips across the back. 'Perhaps
that I want you; that we could be good together.'

Cressida snatched her hand away. 'That's nonsense.
You don't have to flatter me, Lord Dearham.' Her
voice was harsh.

A quick frown appeared. 'Flatter?'

'Yes, flatter. I am my father's daughter, Lord
Dearham. I have heard a lot of flattery in my time and
it doesn't impress me.'

The beautiful mouth quirked. 'You don't sound as if
you have heard any flattery at all,' Rupert pointed out
gently. 'Rather the reverse. Why do you have such a
low opinion of yourself?' He sounded faintly intrigued.

Cressida snatched her hand away. 'What do you
want of me?'

The smile grew. 'If I told you, you'd accuse me of
flattery. I don't think you trust words very much.'

Before she could answer he had pulled her into his
arms. Cressida was aware through every pore of the
texture of his skin, of the even pace of his breathing and
the hammer drive of his heart. And his strength. It was
a long time since she had had a man's strength turned
against her and she had forgotten the instant,
uncontrollable fear that it brought her.

He was not fierce but he brooked no resistance.
Cressida shivered. It was a shock to realise just how
strong he was. The languid, lazy manner was deceptive.
The arms that held her were hard with active muscles.
She felt puny by comparison and very vulnerable.

'You're doing it again,' said Rupert softly into her
hair.

'Doing what?' she faltered.

'Freezing like a threatened rabbit. I don't like it.'

She swallowed. 'Then let me go,' she retorted.

He gave a soft chuckle. 'Where will that get us?' he demanded and then he was kissing her again.

This time Cressida fought strenuously. He was laughing at her. Everything he said, everything he did, made it clear that he found her amusing. It was intolerable; particularly so when he held her caught with that easy strength and refused to listen to her protests. She heaved against his hold with all her strength, hauling her shoulders away and pressing her hands against his chest.

Her resistance made no noticeable impression. With a sudden furious movement, Cressida twisted herself out of his hold and back. But too late she remembered her precarious position. She half fell, half rolled into the stream as the ground gave way on the edge of the bank.

Rupert Dearham was taken by surprise. He made one hopeless grab for her and then flung himself back from the brink in order not to follow her example. He leaped on to the flat millstone where she had originally been sitting and went down on one knee, inspecting her.

'Are you all right?'

Cressida had damaged little but her dignity. She sat up, shaking the sodden hair out of her eyes, and glowered at him. The little stream was very cold and fast but it was not deep and she was sitting on the shingly bottom. The current buffeted her and made her shiver but she was in no danger of being swept away.

Rupert was looking unforgivably amused. He held out a hand.

'Come along. It would be silly to catch cold on a fine summer day like this one.'

Ignoring the hand, Cressida struggled to her feet. The current caught her behind the knees and she staggered. At once Rupert was beside her, his immaculate trousers soaked to the knee, his arms supporting her. Under his guidance she waded not very steadily to the bank and scrambled back on to the grass. She lay there panting as

Rupert put both hands on a flat section of turf and vaulted lightly up beside her. Then he turned to look down at her, the green eyes gleaming.

She glared at him, silently daring him to make some mocking remark. But he only touched her cold cheek with a fingertip and said in a voice of suppressed amusement,

'I think you're out of condition for exploits like that.'

His own breathing, she saw with annoyance, was not even quickened. When she could control her heaving breaths she sat up, not looking at him.

'What are you going to do now?' Rupert asked with odious interest. 'Swing from an apple-tree? Climb the thatched roof?'

Cressida was beginning to shiver as much with reaction as from cold.

'You think you're so funny,' she said resentfully between chattering teeth.

'There is a funny side to it, certainly, and I cannot blind myself to it,' he said, 'even though it isn't particularly good for my image. I don't think a woman has ever launched herself into three feet of icy water to avoid my beastly advances before.'

There was a pregnant pause. Their eyes met: Cressida's furious, Rupert's rueful yet with a hint of that seriousness she had already detected. An icy drip of water launched itself from her chin to trickle between her breasts, making her jump. Seeing it, Rupert's lip quivered.

Suddenly Cressida began to laugh.

'Oh, you're atrocious,' she said when she could speak. She held out an imperative hand to him. 'Help me up and I'll go and make some tea and get into some dry clothes.'

'Very sensible,' he approved, obeying. 'Though aesthetically speaking, a pity.'

He let his eyes wander down her body with blatant

appreciation, making her aware that the soaking shorts and top clung to her every curve. Normally, she would have felt threatened and resentful under such inspection. Today she was too overwhelmed by the shock of icy water and the release of laughter. Though she shook her head at him in remonstrance, she neither tensed nor snatched her hand out of his warm clasp.

They walked back to the cottage hand in hand.

'I'll go and change,' said Cressida, suddenly shy.

She made a great business of filling the kettle and plugging it into the socket above the Aga. It meant that she could avoid looking at Rupert.

'What about you?' she added as an afterthought. 'You're wet too.'

'Not as comprehensively as you. I'll dry out in the sun. Don't worry about me. If I didn't succumb to pneumonia on the ice floes, I'm not going to do it from getting my feet wet in the middle of June.'

Cressida dipped her head in acknowledgement. He was right, obviously. Those expeditions of his, which one forgot so easily because he did not look like the outdoor type, must have made him formidably fit. Murmuring something unintelligible she retreated to her room.

The cottage had only one room upstairs under the sloping roof. Cressida had added a small *en suite* bathroom but otherwise it was exactly as it had been in the seventeenth century when the cottage was first built: exposed beams, uneven, polished wooden floor and windows on all four sides set at an angle to the sloping rafters. Just now it was filled with the late afternoon sun: which, thought Cressida wryly, picked out the cobwebs that had accumulated in her absence, in pretty relief.

It was just as well that Rupert Dearham was not going to penetrate this far to see the evidence of her uninspired housekeeping. Thinking of the circumstances in which Rupert Dearham might venture into her bedroom set her trembling again. Damn the man, why did he take her off balance like this? Why was she aware of him all the time—and aware, too, that he knew it?

She scrambled into a print skirt and frail peasant blouse. It was old and thin with much washing, the drawstrings at the throat and wrists fraying. But it was clean and dry and came easily to hand.

She brushed her hair vigorously. It was already drying, beginning to curl wildly about her face. She tied it back at the nape with a scarf of the same print as her skirt in a vain attempt to quell the riot. She grimaced at her image in the ancient mirror in the corner. It was not how she wanted to look. She looked too young, with the swirling skirt and tumbled hair. Too vulnerable as well, with her mouth still rosy from his kisses. None of it, she was quite certain, would escape Rupert Dearham's lazy observation.

There was nothing to be done, however, She would have to go downstairs, face him. Perhaps when she had given him tea he would go. She squared her shoulders. She was fairly certain that he would not leave until he had done what he came to do and so far she had no idea of what that might be. Well, there was only one way to find out.

The kitchen was empty. The kettle was steaming. Clearly it had boiled and been switched off. Cressida looked out of the kitchen window and saw Rupert settled on the grass as if he had been lounging on her lawns all his life. Beside him was a tray bearing cups, jugs and the teapot. He had made himself very much at home in the short time she had spent dressing. She bit her lip. It made her feel invaded.

Cressida marched out to him with resolution.

'What are you doing here, Lord Dearham?'

He did not answer for a moment, pouring out tea into a mug instead and handing it up to her. She accepted it automatically.

'Taking afternoon tea with a charming lady,' he replied.

She brushed it aside. 'No. Your *real* reason for coming here.'

His eyes did not waver. He said soberly, 'I had the feeling—last night—that I had hurt you really badly. I hope—I have hoped all day—that I was mistaken. I had to find out.'

Cressida sank down nervelessly to the grass beside him.

'And have you?' she asked in a strained voice.

'In part, yes. I think I have.'

'And?'

There was a silence in which Cressida felt her nerves knot themselves tight.

When he spoke it was with apparent irrelevance. 'Have you always worked for your father?'

She stared at him blankly. 'Yes.'

'And are you happy doing so?'

She bristled. 'As happy as I would be doing anything else.'

'Does he often give you the sort of orders I overheard in New York?'

She was taken by surprise. She felt the shamed colour rise into her face uncontrollably. She turned her head away, unable to meet his eyes.

Rupert said with sudden roughness, 'Don't look like that. It's not your fault. And as you pointed out last night, I did not overhear your agreeing. I'm just trying to understand.'

'Understand what?' said Cressida in a muffled voice.

'You, of course,' he said, as if she should have already realised it, as if it were obvious. 'That's why I came down here. I had to know whether your sudden flight to sanctuary was because you were afraid of me.'

Although she could not look him in the eye, Cressida was watching his hands. She now saw to her astonishment that they were clenched tight, so that the knuckles stood out. He seemed to be waiting for her answer in coiled tension, as if he in his turn were afraid.

She said gently, 'Not entirely.'

The long powerful fingers dug into the grass. 'But in part.'

She could not deny it. Fear of him had run through her like wine, not since last night but since the first time she had set eyes on him. From that very first moment she had recognised him as a danger to her peace of mind.

'It's all my own fault, I suppose, my damned temper.'

Cressida frowned, puzzled. 'Temper?'

Rupert was wry. 'Another inherited trait, I'm afraid. The Dearhams have been known for it for centuries. One of them is supposed to have been banished from Gloriana's court for losing his temper and beating up a courtier. A favoured courtier, so the story goes. The Dearhams have never been known for their discrimination, either.'

Cressida remembered his firm hands on her skin, the amused assurance, the absolute self-possession.

'Are you telling me you were in a temper last night?' she said incredulously. 'I would never have guessed it.'

He said, 'I was very angry.'

'But—but why? And when?'

'From the moment I realised you had flown back specially to stage-manage that dinner party. It seemed to me that you and your father were both taking altogether too much for granted.'

She shook her head, the unconfined curls wafting while the scarf slipped lower down her ponytail. 'I don't understand.'

'No?' Rupert's voice was bitter. 'Can you deny you had me written off as an expensive playboy before ever we got to that acquisition meeting?'

Cressida said firmly, 'I knew virtually nothing about

you. I didn't have you written off as anything. I can't speak for my father, of course.' The fugitive smile appeared. 'But then he tends to despise the whole of the younger generation, so if he doesn't have much respect for you, you're hardly alone in that.'

'Does he think the whole of the younger generation can be bribed by the sexual attentions of his daughter?' Rupert demanded savagely.

'Ah,' said Cressida, as enlightenment dawned. She looked down at her hands, choosing her words carefully. 'The trouble is that Papa also has a temper which he loses too easily.' She hesitated. 'And on this occasion he did not lose it with you but with me.'

Rupert's eyes narrowed. He did not speak.

She went on bravely, 'If he really thought that—er—sexual attentions would have any influence on your decision, he certainly wouldn't have proposed me for the job.' She twined her fingers together, watching them absorbedly. 'He doesn't have much of an opinion of my powers of attraction.' In which, she remembered painfully, he was not alone. 'I'm surprised you didn't overhear that as well. He was quite clear on the subject.'

Rupert said in a whisper, 'What do you mean?'

Cressida ran her tongue over her dry lips. She had never talked this frankly to anyone before. She would not be doing it now if it were not somehow desperately important that Rupert Dearham should not think she despised him. Suddenly that seemed the most important thing in the world, more important by far even than her own carefully guarded privacy.

'My father blames me for the break-up of my marriage,' she said flatly. 'He was very attached to my ex-husband, you see. Keith was a sort of elected heir-apparent. When we divorced, all that was spoilt, I suppose. Papa thinks it was my fault. He has never forgiven me.'

The silence stretched between them. Cressida could hear the humming of bees, the rustle of small creatures in the grass, the distant splashing of the stream against its banks. Rupert was very still. He had half turned towards her, resting on one elbow, his long legs stretched out in front of him. He was not looking at her. His head was bent. The low sun struck gold from his gleaming head. The handsome profile was in shadow. He looked remote, brooding, unapproachable.

Cressida said on a note of desperation, 'Please, you *must* believe me. It was me he wanted to hurt, not you.'

The golden head rose slowly. 'It seems I owe you even more of an apology than I thought.'

Cressida shrugged. 'It's hardly your fault.'

'No? But if I had not been who I am—with the reputation I have earned—he would not have used my presence to insult you in such a way.'

Cressida met his eyes. Although he sounded calm, even resigned, his eyes were bitter. She was bewildered and more than a little disturbed. He was not at all what she had expected before she met him, nor yet anything like the character given him by the gossip columnists. She felt unwillingly sympathetic.

She said, 'My father would have insulted me anyway. He was in that sort of mood. And besides——' She bit it off. No, she was not going to give away all her secrets, not to Rupert Dearham. He might be less shallow than his publicity gave him credit for but he was still largely an unknown quantity. She would be very unwise to pour into his ears an account of her conversation that morning with her father and her fears that Keith Harley was about to return to her life. It slightly frightened her that she should want to.

Rupert did not press her, though the look he gave her was shrewd.

All he did was to say, with another of his startling

changes of subject, 'What does your mother think of the way your father pushes you around?'

That was easy. Cressida smiled in relief.

'My mother died years ago. In fact, I'm not sure I remember her. I was more or less brought up by Marthe.'

Rupert's eyes narrowed. He persisted, 'So what does Marthe think of it?'

Cressida was surprised. It had not occurred to her to wonder. Though now she came to think of it, Marthe had told her that very morning.

'She said I was too good to him,' she reported literally, unwary in her discovery.

'She sounds like a shrewd lady,' observed Rupert. He sat up clasping his knees, looking at her soberly. 'Do you have to work for him? Has he some hold over you, some contract?'

Cressida was slightly shocked. 'He's my father.'

Rupert's mouth twisted. 'I have a father too, but I don't see him from one year's end to the next. And if he ever spoke to me the way Jerome Sebastian spoke to you, he'd never see me again.'

There was a pause.

At last Cressida said slowly, 'I'm all the family he has. I'm very important to him.'

'It sounded like it,' said Rupert sarcastically.

'No, you don't understand. I'm a disappointment. I should have been a boy.' She smiled faintly. 'If not several boys. My father was an orphan and a refugee. He would have liked a big family. But my mother was delicate and he never wanted to marry anyone else. So——' she shrugged. 'He had to make do with me.'

Rupert's face wore an odd expression. 'And that's the tale he brought you up on?'

Cressida said, 'It's no tale. It's the truth.'

He rose to his feet. His voice surged with anger. 'Truth or not, he had no right to lay that on a child.

The man is a monster. God knows, I thought my family were frightful but they're a fairy-tale compared with your papa. How dare he? How *dare* he?'

Cressida stared up at him, torn between amazement and affront. Rupert swung round on her.

'Shall I tell you about my family? I'm an only child too. I get the title and the estates and God knows how many people will depend on me when I do. I don't get any money to run the place or pay their wages, though. It will all have gone by then. My father will have lost it on the horses or the baccarat tables. When he dies the estate will have to be sold. Families who have worked for us for generations will be sold out with it.'

Cressida sat very still, impressed by the raw pain and fury in his voice.

'Do you know what that means? It means I'm unemployable and always have been. Everybody knows I'll inherit—though they don't know that I'll be unable to keep to it—so what is the point of them taking me on and training me? I'll only leave to go back to the country and take my rightful place doing my proper job, one day.' He gave a harsh laugh. 'In the meantime they expect me to be a playboy. It's a long Dearham tradition, that.'

She stared at him before saying coolly, 'But you're not.'

The green eyes glinted. 'Not entirely, perhaps.'

'Playboys go on Geographical Society expeditions?' she asked in tones of faint interest. 'Playboys lecture on botany and write books about it?'

Rupert gave a crack of laughter. 'No, that was my escape. Salvation by fungus. I know more about Amazon mushrooms than you're ever going to want to learn.'

'And what about the company Papa wanted to buy from you? You were clearly involved in that.'

'Ah yes, Queen Anne Place.' He shrugged. 'I started

a business years ago, when I was still at Cambridge, with some friends. It was a sort of uncomfortable tours operator. We would take people to the Iguassu Falls the hard way, if you follow me. It's amazing how many people like to do it like that. The company grew of course and at one point it acquired a little publishing house. We want to keep the imprint that does travel books and reference works but there's not much point in our hanging on to the language publications side. It doesn't fit in with what we do.'

'Then why wouldn't you sell it to Papa?' asked Cressida, genuinely intrigued. 'If he was offering you a good price for something you wanted to sell anyway?'

Rupert's face closed at once. 'I didn't come here to talk business.'

'I wasn't,' Cressida protested. 'Anyone would have asked the same.'

'Would they?' His eyes were guarded now. All the disarming warmth had gone as if it had been wiped off a slate. Cressida felt chilled. Perhaps it had all been an illusion in the first place. Perhaps it was just another facet of his famous charm, the ability to give that illusion that he was confiding in you. She drew back slightly.

'It is the obvious comment,' she informed him.

'Obvious to hot-shot businesswomen maybe.'

She stood up, brushing grass from her skirt. She was in full retreat now. 'But that is what I am,' she reminded him sweetly. 'You knew that when you decided to come down here.'

'Yes, I suppose I did.' Outrageously, he sounded disappointed.

Cressida returned their mugs to the tray and picked it up.

'It's getting late.'

He took the tray from her with practised courtesy.

'Hardly,' he said, with an ironical look in the

direction of the sun. The evening sky was streaked with flame and the shadows on the grass had lengthened but it was still light and Cressida had to admit that it would be so for more than two hours.

She said with her best social smile, 'I'm sure you have arrangements for this evening. It takes about an hour and a half to get back to town.'

Rupert smiled calmly. 'I'll remember that.'

He took the tray into the kitchen, Cressida following in his wake trying to repress burgeoning anxiety.

'Do you mean you're *not* going back to London this evening?'

'No,' he agreed, shouldering open the kitchen door and side-stepping the attentions of the junior cat who had returned for supper. His smile mocked her.

'You're going on somewhere else?' she asked, without much hope.

'No.'

She was by now thoroughly agitated. She knew it was a mistake but she rushed into speech, unable to fence with him.

'You can't stay here.'

Rupert set down the tray on the kitchen table and turned to look at her. His good humour seemed to be completely restored. When he spoke his voice was gentle, even reasonable.

'And how do you propose to stop me?'

CHAPTER FIVE

THE telephone shrilled into the taut silence, shocking them both. Cressida jumped and stood frozen. Rupert watched her.

'Don't you usually answer your telephone?'

Reluctantly she nodded and went to the instrument on the kitchen wall. She picked it up in something akin to dread.

'Yes?'

'Is that you?' asked Lesley Button, sounding worried. 'Cressida, are you all right?'

She swallowed. 'Yes.'

Lesley was obviously not reassured. 'You're sure? You're——' she broke off, apparently struck by a thought. 'Are you alone?'

'No,' said Cressida, willing herself not to look at Rupert.

'Oh God, he's found you already. He was here, almost as soon as you'd gone. I told him you were off on a holiday but he did not believe me and he told me he'd track you down wherever you were. I didn't think he could do it this quickly.'

'Yes.'

'And you're sure you're all right? Did you know he was here, then?'

Cressida frowned. 'Here?'

'In England.'

'But surely we both knew. We had dinner last night.' Cressida's voice trailed into silence. A horrid thought struck her. 'Who are you talking about, Lesley?'

'Mr Harley, of course,' said her secretary impatiently. 'I thought you said he was there with you.'

Cressida felt suddenly hollow. 'No. No, not Keith.'

Out of the corner of her eye she saw Rupert's head lift, turn alertly in her direction, though he had seemed to be concentrating on tickling the cat behind its ear, and quite oblivious of her conversation.

'Well, thank God for that,' said Lesley in undisguised relief. 'Whoever he is keep him there. Mr Harley was in a funny sort of mood.'

Cressida thanked her slowly and she rang off. Rupert continued to woo the cat, not looking at her.

'Keith?' he asked casually.

She did not answer. She went to the kitchen rocking chair and sank into it. Her face was very pale.

'Keith who? Keith Harley maybe?'

Cressida's lips felt anaesthetised, as if they were out of her control. They moved but she made no sound.

'Your ex-husband is coming here?' Rupert probed.

She tried to say that it was none of his business. She tried to tell him to leave at once and stop digging into her private life. She tried to find a pithy phrase that would send him sweeping out of her life for ever.

To her horror she burst into tears.

At once Rupert abandoned the cat. He came and knelt before her, pressing a smartly ironed sweet-smelling handkerchief into her hand. He did not touch her or say anything but he did not move away either.

Cressida soaked his handkerchief in a matter of minutes. Once she had started she did not seem as if she could stop. All the tension of the last few days, the anxiety over her father, the punishing business schedule, the unresolved personal conflicts, seemed to well up into a great wave and break over her. She could never remember having cried like it.

She said as much when, after mopping her last tears away and swallowing hard, she returned his handkerchief to him.

'I'm sorry. I don't usually turn into a waterfall at

the touch of a button.'

'No, I don't imagine you do,' Rupert agreed. He pocketed the handkerchief. 'So you'd better tell me what's wrong.''

Cressida sniffed again. 'Oh, no, I'll be all right now.'

'I very much doubt that. And these are obviously very particular circumstances. If you don't tell someone, you'll crack up. It might as well be me.'

In the end he took her to the village pub. All her resistance had been knocked out of her by the successive crises. She felt almost grateful to him for imposing the decision on her. She washed her face, combed her hair out, abandoning the confining scarf, and collected a shawl against the possibility of an evening breeze. Then they walked down the lane and across the village green to the Bear and Ragged Staff.

It was not a pretty pub or a fashionable one. It had serviceable scrubbed wooden tables and stools and a businesslike dartboard in the public bar. At this hour it was virtually deserted. Rupert took their drinks out into the late sunshine and set them on a bench overlooking the village green. Some schoolchildren were playing a raggedy game of cricket.

'This is a nice place,' said Rupert with approval, stretching his legs in front of him in evident contentment. 'You were very clever to find it.'

'Lucky,' Cressida corrected him.

She had washed away the tear-stains and was now in command of herself but she was still subdued.

'But perhaps cleverness is no more than recognising when you're lucky.'

Cressida sighed. 'Are you telling me I ought to be grateful for my lot?'

Rupert sank lower on the bench, his hands in his pockets.

'That would be very presumptuous of me,' he drawled. 'Especially when I don't know anything about your lot.

Or at any rate not very much. Keith Harley, for example.'

Her fingers tightened on her glass, though she managed by a supreme effort of will not to flinch. Since she became managing director of Sebastian UK Cressida had had to deal with some tough personal battles. Nothing had ever intimidated her as much as the thought of facing a remorseful Keith backed by the full barrage of support from Jerome.

Rupert was watching the children, his eye lazy under down-dropped lids. Nevertheless, he must have noticed her tell-tale reaction because he asked sardonically, 'Did he beat you?'

Cressida jumped and sat up straighter on her bench, 'Of course not. I should have left him.'

'But you did,' pointed out the soft voice.

'No.' For a moment she said no more. Then she braced herself. Perhaps he was right, perhaps she had been bottling it up for too long. Perhaps Keith's desertion would not have hurt for so long if she had talked about it in the first place. She ran her tongue over her lips. 'He left me. For a blonde computer programmer in Santa Monica.'

'Ah!' He nodded, as if it were the answer to some not very important crossword clue.

'I thought they would get married. God knows why they didn't. And now Papa says they have broken up.'

'And he wants you back.' It was not a question.

'My Papa would like it to happen like that, certainly.' Cressida was wry.

'And you?' He lit a cigarette. Cressida was surprised. She did not recall seeing him smoke before. 'What do you think about it? After all, you've never remarried either. Perhaps you still think of yourself as his wife.'

'No,' she said positively.

'Of course six years is a long time,' Rupert observed in a reflective voice.

'It has nothing to do with time,' Cressida interrupted.

She leaned forward, suddenly reckless. 'The marriage was over long before Keith left me.'

The green eyes lifted, considered her dispassionately and then were veiled again as he transferred his gaze to the game on the green.

'Tell,' he invited softly.

And suddenly, startlingly, she did. She found herself talking freely to him as she had never done to Keith; talking about the strange disjointed childhood when she was alternately banished behind a green baize door with a succession of nannies or dressed up years ahead of her age and paraded before guests; talking of her affection for her father and her worry about his increasingly frenetic lifestyle; about her isolation, her unused talents, her fears; and, at last, her marriage.

'Keith was sort of picked out for me while I was still an adolescent,' she said in a low voice. Her drink stood untouched. 'I didn't realise, of course. He used to come on holidays with us. Later on, he would escort me to dances, parties, that sort of thing. When I went to university he used to come and see me every other weekend. And he was always telephoning.' She passed a hand over her brow. 'You'll think I'm very stupid but it genuinely never occurred to me that there was something weird in a successful man in his late twenties dancing attendance on a schoolgirl. Which was what I was, in effect. The other girls had boyfriends. That's what I thought Keith was: an ordinary boyfriend.'

'But he was extraordinary?' Rupert asked politely, as she fell silent.

Cressida flushed. 'Well, in a way.'

'What way?'

She bit her lip, not answering.

'Let me guess,' said Rupert with gentle irony. 'Sex.'

The bright head dipped. 'Yes.'

'And of course you're not exactly a free spirit even now. Did he frighten you?'

She shook her head violently. 'No. You don't understand. It wasn't like that.'

'So explain,' he urged gently.

'He never seemed interested in—that side of things.'

'*What?*' She had at last succeeded in startling him, Cressida thought bitterly.

'No. Oh, he'd kiss me, you know, whenever he was obliged to, but he never tried to get me into bed or anything, not even when we were engaged.' She turned her head blindly, concentrating on the small figures on the green through the film of recalled tears. 'You'll think I'm stupid: I thought it was because he was so much older and sex didn't matter to him so much any more. I knew he was different in that respect from my friends' boyfriends and I just thought it was because he was steady and sober and ambitious and hadn't got time for that sort of thing.'

'You were wrong?'

'On every count. Well, I was right with ambitious, maybe.' She paused before saying hardly, 'He wasn't attracted to me. I don't think he even liked me. But he was attracted to inheriting the Sebastian chairmanship and he and my Papa were crazy about each other.'

'When did he tell you this?' Rupert's voice was even. 'After you were married presumably?'

Cressida moved her shoulders. 'It came out by degrees over time. I'd been too sheltered as a teenager. I grew up fast after I married.'

The beautiful mouth turned into a thin line. 'And just the way a father wants his only daughter to grow up. Did Jerome force you to stay together?'

She shook her head. 'Not me. He may have said something to Keith, of course. He must have known about Keith's women. Just about everyone in the company did.'

'Including you?'

She was surprised. 'Oh yes. He used to tell me about them.'

'*Tell* you!'

'He—got to hate me. I wasn't—you see—well,' she gave him a swift, self-mocking smile, 'you said it yourself, just now: I'm not exactly a free spirit. According to Keith, at first I clung too much. Then in the end I couldn't bring myself to cling at all. So his revenge was to come home and tell me about the women a man *enjoyed* making love to.'

'Dear sweet God,' Rupert said very softly.

'So you see I don't feel as if I'm still married to him. In a way, I feel as if we never were married; as if it was a horrible, sordid, adolescent affair.'

His face took on a grimmer expression than she would have imagined possible.

'And this man is coming here? Isn't that what you were told on the telephone?'

Cressida shuddered. 'He may not be able to find me,' she said without much conviction.

Rupert brushed it aside. 'I found you.'

'Yes,' she admitted. 'I keep trying not to remember that.'

He gave a theatrical wince. 'Ouch.'

She looked up, startled, her eyes crinkling at his expression. 'Oh, I'm sorry, I didn't mean it the way it sounded.' She gave him her shy, warm smile that so few people were privileged to see. 'I'm very grateful to you. You've helped enormously being here.'

'Have I?' He was enigmatic. 'I rather doubt it. But, you know, I think I could help. If you wanted.'

Cressida was puzzled and it showed. 'I don't follow?'

'No?' His mouth twisted slightly. 'Look at it from your ex-husband's point of view. From your father's, if you like. They both see no reason why they shouldn't bully you, because they think you're unattached.'

Cressida shook her head in bewilderment. 'So?'

'So attach yourself,' Rupert advised calmly. 'To me.'

The brown eyes got rounder and rounder as she

stared at him, silenced by the enormity of the suggestion.

'Don't look like that,' he said, amused. 'I'm not suggesting anything irreversible. Just a brief public affair to repel your enemies.' He gave an ironic laugh. 'I'm peculiarly well qualified, as far as the publicity goes, at least.'

She said, 'But I can't—you—it's out of the question.'

'Why?'

In a rush of desperation she said, 'Because I don't have affairs. I don't like them.'

He considered that in silence for a moment.

'You're a grown-up, independent woman. You're free. You've been married. Nobody will be hurt if you have a brief fling with me. And we're not exactly unattracted. I don't see the objection.'

'*I* object. I don't care for casual sex.'

'Casual?' he echoed. 'I——'

But she interrupted him. 'All right,' she said in a goaded voice, 'I don't like sex. I never did—it was one of Keith's chief complaints against me—and I don't suppose I'm about to change now.'

She braced herself for his reply. He might laugh. He had laughed at her before and God knew it was a childish enough problem. Or he might not believe her and try to persuade her. At the thought of the form his persuasion might take, Cressida swallowed convulsively. Or he might despise her.

When he spoke it was completely unpredictable. 'I see,' he said slowly, as if he had just been presented with an interesting problem.

'*Please* don't say that I don't know what I'm talking about. Or that I'll get over it,' begged Cressida. The only person that she had confided that particular secret to was Dandy Cartwright, who had refused to take it seriously, offering both those palliatives.

'No, I won't say that,' Rupert said absently.

'But you do see that it makes your scheme impossible? Though I'm very grateful for the suggestion of course.' Cressida sighed. 'It would have been the perfect answer,' she said with unconscious wistfulness.

Rupert sat up, suddenly brisk. 'And it still is. We can just as easily tell the papers we are having an affair without going to the lengths of making it true.' He flashed her a disarming grin. 'It's not as much fun, of course, but it could still do the trick as far as your oppressors are concerned.'

Cressida was awed. 'Tell a lie, you mean?'

He shrugged. 'Oh, we needn't do that. We could tell the truth. And then just refuse to say any more and disappear together for a week. In fact,' he added thoughtfully, 'we're already ideally placed to be found in a sinful episode.'

She shivered. 'I don't like the idea. What would people think?'

'What would your ex-husband think?' Rupert countered.

She was tempted. 'I—oh, I can't decide. You must give me time.'

Rupert smiled. 'How much time will your ex-husband give you?'

Cressida closed her eyes. 'Well, he won't be here tonight. I'll think about it tonight.'

'Whatever you say.' Rupert leaned forward as if he were about to touch her, then seemed to think better of it, halting. 'I am at your service. Whenever you want. And anyway, one day we must talk about this marriage of yours.'

Cressida laughed. 'You already know all there is to know. I've spilled every last bean.'

Rupert did not smile. 'No, you haven't. There is at least one thing you haven't told me. The most important thing.' And seeing her dawning apprehension he went on, 'No, I won't ask you now. But one day I will. And you'll have to tell me.'

After that, Cressida found that she felt oddly at ease with him. It was as if he had known her all her life and she did not have to disguise her weaker or her nastier sides from him. It was extraordinarily relaxing. Walking home through the star-filled night she told him so.

'Thank you,' he said gravely. 'I hope that doesn't mean I've bored you to tears.'

Cressida gave a ripple of laughter. 'I said relaxing, not soporific,' she assured him. 'And you're the one who is most likely to have been bored.' She took his arm confidingly. 'You have the gift of listening, do you know that?'

Rupert covered her hand with his own and held it in a light, warm clasp.

'Only to the right people.'

'You mean the ones who talk too much?' she asked wryly and was surprised when he stopped dead.

'There you go again,' he said. 'Denigrating yourself. What is it with you, Cressida? Why are you always putting yourself down?'

Her eyes widened. 'I didn't know I did.'

'No?' Rupert resumed walking, a frown between his brows. 'I noticed it at once, even in New York. You didn't say much but what you said was either to the point or—' he shrugged, 'denigrating yourself, as I said. It puzzled me. It seemed to undermine your own arguments; and your arguments were good. I had you down as a very bright lady.'

'Had?'

'Oh, don't misunderstand me. I'm still sure you're a whizz-kid in the Board Room and in the office. It's just in personal encounters that you're like this, isn't it?'

Not knowing how to answer him, Cressida stayed silent.

'I had a dog once,' mused Rupert. 'A pointer. Terribly well bred. My father gave him to me because he thought he was the sort of dog I ought to have. He was like you. If we met another dog on our walks, he would just keel over with all four paws in the air. It was surrender, you see. Sometimes before the other dog was even close enough to attack.'

'He sounds pretty much of a coward,' Cressida observed in a carefully neutral voice.

Rupert was smiling reminiscently. 'The biggest coward I've ever met. He was my best friend for years.' He flashed her a wicked grin. 'I adore cowards. They make me feel protective.'

'You think I'm a coward?' she said, uncertain whether she was amused or not.

Rupert considered. 'No, not in all circumstances, certainly not. But sometimes——' he broke off. 'Well, what do you think?'

'*I* think,' Cressida said with irony, 'that I know myself well enough to know my weak points. If I point them out, it's only because I like to get in first. It's less painful than having them pointed out for you.'

'Ah.' Rupert was silent for a moment. 'Yes, I had not thought of that. Of course, you do have a permanent judge and jury in the family, only too willing to point out your weaknesses, don't you?'

Cressida was in a quandary. Family loyalty urged her to say that he misjudged her father. Professional loyalty—and after all, Rupert Dearham was still a business rival, refusing to sell a company that Jerome Sebastian had set his heart on—argued that she should defend Sebastian's judgement to the last. Native honesty kept her silent.

'Very wise,' he murmured, apparently reading her mind, she thought with irritation. 'I shouldn't have believed you if you denied it.' He stopped again and turned her to face him. They were in the lane leading to her cottage, under a delicate silver birch which leaned over the hedge in the far corner of her garden. Behind the tracery of branches and gently wafting leaves, Cressida could see the stars above his head. Rupert held her by the shoulders and looked intently into her face.

'I'll tell you one thing, Cressida Harley,' he said in a strange voice. 'On the whole I think I do believe what you tell me. And that is a very rare thing for me where a woman is concerned. No——' as she moved restlessly and his hands tightened '——no, don't move. And don't tell me I'm flattering you either, or I shall shake you. I don't flatter my friends. And I do, very much, want to be your friend, Cressida. I think you could do with one. And I know I could.'

Cressida held her breath. She was aware that not just the conversation, the whole encounter with Rupert Dearham had shifted to a new plane. In spite of his teasing, she sensed a deep seriousness in him, as if he were reaching out to her at a level infinitely more profound than that of her everyday relationships.

It was exhilarating, she found, but also slightly nerve-racking. She did not know what to say, how to respond. She did not know what was expected of her. Nor did she know what she wanted to. All that she knew was that she had an unaccustomed and highly unexpected urge to turn to Rupert in confidence and friendship, notwithstanding his reputation and her own inner warnings. And yet, and yet . . .

She said carefully at last, 'But you have lots of friends. I'm told you're very popular.'

The fine mouth compressed. 'Don't be trivial. You know that's not what I mean.'

She stared at the ground absorbedly. 'Then what?'

'Oh, not an affair either, since you're so set against it.' He sounded impatient. 'But you and I——' he hesitated. 'We have things to give each other, I think. And perhaps we both need to give.'

It struck a chord. 'It's a long time since I've been asked to give anything,' Cressida said sombrely.

Rupert's eyes lit with laughter, dispelling the mood. 'Except total subservience to your father,' he observed wryly. 'And I'm not after subservience.'

He took her hand, turning it over between both of his, inspecting its ringless pallor. His face was remote, unreadable.

At last he said, 'So shall we strike a bargain, Cressida? Friendship?'

Her fingers moved in his. She felt a glow, soft and secret and utterly new, begin to steal through her. She smiled shyly, direct into his eyes.

'It's a bargain.'

They shook hands solemnly in the twilight. Then they walked on in companionable silence. At the garden gate, Rupert paused, unlatching it, and held it open for Cressida to pass in front of him. She looked at him enquiringly.

'No, I won't come in. But I'll see you tomorrow. Early.'

'You're staying in the district?' Cressida asked, puzzled. It was not a short drive from London.

Rupert was enigmatic. 'We'll see. Anyway, tomorrow we have to talk about your operation to repel boarders.' And as she continued to look bemused he added softly, reminding her, 'Harley.'

Instinctively she shivered in a reaction she was not quick enough to repress. Rupert's eyes narrowed but he did not comment.

She said as lightly as she could manage, 'From what I can gather you thought it would be a better idea if it were *your* operation.'

He did not touch her. He did not move. But she felt as if he had put his arms round her, warm and comforting.

'Yes,' he said gently. 'Yes.'

Her eyes flew to his face. She hesitated. 'I don't know, Rupert,' she said in troubled voice. 'It would mean living a lie. And not just for the newspapers, whatever you might say. We'd have to deceive a lot of people. Even if I wanted to I'm not sure I'm that good an actress.'

'You'd rather handle Harley alone and unaided?' he asked coolly.

'I——' Cressida bit her lip. 'You don't understand,' she said at last, despairingly. 'I'm *used* to handling things alone and unaided.'

Rupert smiled suddenly, his eyes full of an unexpected tenderness.

'So I'm offering a whole new experience. You might enjoy it. Anyway,' he paused as if he might kiss her and then, abruptly, took a pace backwards. 'Think about it. I'll be around tomorrow early. You can give me your answer then.'

CHAPTER SIX

THE next few days were, Cressida often thought afterwards, the oddest and yet the most important of her life. She led a weird, dreamlike existence in which she seemed to be two quite separate people. The first was the old, cool Cressida. She talked to Lesley on the telephone daily, received mail and took decisions just as she was used to doing. Lesley, as far as she could tell, detected no change in her absent employer.

The rest of the time, however, she was in turmoil. She washed and polished and gardened frantically. She spent long hours making grandiose and quite unrealisable plans about a new start to her suddenly unsatisfactory life. She wrote letters to personal friends, some of which had been put off since Christmas. And she failed, signally, to make any decision at all about Rupert Dearham.

She saw him every day. She did not know where he was staying but as he had promised he arrived early, usually for breakfast. The first day she told him, gently, that she could not agree to a pretended affair with him. And he told her, gently, that she should take more time to think about it. In the meantime they should take the opportunity to cement their newly declared friendship.

Cressida felt as if she were being swept along before a force infinitely greater than she had ever encountered before. She could not account for this. Rupert was charming, witty and delightful company. She felt at peace with him. He did not browbeat her or hector her or try to blackmail her by playing on her feelings of gratitude. And yet there was something—a certain dogged persistence under the lazy smile and casual manner—which left her with the feeling that she had never had the last word. That the decision, if decision there was, had still to be taken and would probably not be taken by her.

To one who was used to running her life as she chose, it was a bewildering feeling. Cressida was not sure she liked it. Indeed, there were times when she was not sure she liked Lord Dearham, either. He had a way of withdrawing into his own thoughts sometimes which made her feel suspicious. Perhaps his offer of friendship, though it had seemed straightforward enough, was no more than a blind. Perhaps he was using all that famous charm to play upon her, so that she might be induced to use her influence with her father to ... But at that point her suspicions fell over themselves. Lord Dearham had no interest in influencing Jerome Sebastian. He did not want anything from him. On the contrary, it was Jerome who wanted Rupert's publishing house.

So perhaps, Cressida would conclude wryly, Rupert in his turn was subconsciously suspicious of her motives. She, after all, had obviously a great deal more to gain commercially from their unlikely truce.

If he did harbour any such thoughts, he did not show it. He was charm itself, teasing her into accompanying him on riverside rambles or, sighing, allowing himself to be pressed into weeding the vegetable patch.

'You know, high-powered executives are not supposed to live on home-grown spinach,' Rupert complained on their third day.

Cressida was collecting windfalls in the orchard, accompanied by the cats.

'Nonsense,' she called back to him, amused. 'Think of Popeye.'

Rupert leaned on his fork and regarded her balefully. 'Popeye didn't look like Meissen porcelain, think like a computer and get other people to do his digging for him.'

Cressida threw a small fallen Worcester Pearmain at him. 'It's good for you.'

The cats, sensing a game, crouched hopefully down in the long orchard grass. Rupert fielded the apple neatly and tossed it back at her. Both cats streaked after it. Abandoning his fork, Rupert strolled lazily up the incline towards her.

'That I'm beginning to doubt,' he said drily and when she looked puzzled said, 'never mind. Skip it. How much of the kitchen garden do you really want dug up?'

Cressida looked past him at the sizeable patch of fruit and vegetables. In only three days he had turned over the earth in two-thirds of it. In spite of his mocking protestations that he was exhausted, he had seemed to be tireless. She had watched in awe as, shirtless and cheerful, he had shifted weeds and cement-dry earth in a steady rhythm that betrayed neither effort nor weariness. Cressida had watched the powerful muscles in his shoulders bunch and release, bunch and release, recognising with an odd shiver that she had been right when she had thought how very strong he was.

She said now, 'I don't often get such willing help. It would break my heart to turn down a good offer.'

Rupert grinned. 'I'll remind you of that one day,' he told her, leering horribly.

'Oh!' She pretended to start back like some oppressed heroine from a silent movie.

Rupert managed to give a sinister laugh and continued inexorably up the hill. Mock-terrified, Cressida lobbed another expendable windfall on him and, with little chirrups of glee, the cats launched themselves after it from their hiding-place.

Taking an apple in the chest, a cat at the ankle and threatened by the war cries of the junior cat, Rupert staggered and stopped dead. Cressida burst into laughter. The senior cat, a persistent rather than intelligent animal, continued to retreat and pounce on

Rupert's ankle for the space of several seconds before discovering that this was not his quarry. Rupert picked him up gently and settled him over his shoulder, tickling him behind the ear.

'So it is war,' he said, glaring at Cressida over the top of a now purring bundle of grey fur. 'You set your familiars on me, do you, witch?'

'Oh, stop it,' begged Cressida, clutching her side. 'I've got a stitch. Don't make me laugh any more.'

'*Laugh?*' he echoed in outrage. He strode towards her, pausing only to tip the senior cat gently into the undergrowth. 'I'll teach you to laugh at me, you hussy!'

And he was before her, eyes sparkling, pulling her into his arms while she still shook with laughter. And suddenly everything changed. The laughter stilled in her throat, though not with alarm. A deep sense of rightness filled her. She watched him steadily, half smiling, as his hands took hold of her slim shoulders, moved, accommodated themselves to the length of her spine, her elegant waist, the soft swell of her hips.

Rupert took her chin firmly in one long-fingered hand and made her look up at him.

'Well, witch, have you put a spell on me?' he demanded softly.

Cressida's lips parted in mute answer. He caught his breath.

'You are gorgeous,' Rupert said, hardly above a whisper.

Of their own independent will, it seemed, her hands went up behind his neck, her fingers interlacing in the silky smooth hair. She rose to her toes, urging his head down. Very, very slowly, he complied with her unspoken plea.

The kiss was long and breathless. Cressida could feel not just his mouth but the whole of his body burning into her flesh. She felt as if she were melting, only to be remodelled in order to fit against his bones and muscles and beating blood. His hands on her hips were like steel, infinitely strong and sensitive. His breath filled her mouth. She could hear nothing but the sledgehammer of his heart. Every sense was unbearably, exquisitely alive to him. When he raised his head, she shrank closer to him.

Rupert looked down at her, a tender, rueful smile on the fine mouth. He stroked her hair with a hand that was not quite steady, winding an auburn curl round his finger and holding it up to the sunlight.

'Rupert——' she said in an undervoice. It was another plea and they both knew it. Only Cressida did not know what she was pleading for.

'For a lady who doesn't want an affair, you have the oddest way of getting your message across,' he said, something almost like pain in his voice.

Cressida stared at him. Slowly the world righted itself. Her breathing slowed. She heard the birds and the splashing of the brook again, smelled the sun-filled grasses and saw the old cottage; saw, too, Rupert's handsome, enigmatic face. She could not read his expression. His eyes were veiled by the steep lids. The sensual mouth was twisted mockingly.

Slowly Cressida removed herself from his arms.

'I'm sorry.'

'Yes,' Rupert agreed, almost savagely. 'I dare say you are.'

'I didn't mean——'

'No,' he interrupted her. 'No. I know. And be thankful I recognised it.'

She swallowed, feeling off balance and helpless. This was the antithesis of the Cressida Harley who had spoken so decisively only that morning to Lesley Button. She pushed her hair back from her hot face.

'Please listen to me,' she began but was interrupted again, this time by a shout from the stream.

'Damn!' she said with concentrated fury, recognising Vic and his dog coming along the bank towards them.

Rupert, by contrast, relaxed visibly. He cast her an amused glance from under the down-dropped lids, once again the teasing sophisticate.

'Inopportune, I agree. But hardly worth your ill-wishing the poor chap, my little witch.'

He strolled down the raked lawns to meet Vic, whom he had met a couple of times already. More slowly Cressida followed, her basket of windfalls on her arm. The cats danced and darted along beside her.

When she reached the men she knew at once that something was wrong. Rupert, no longer lazy, was looking remarkably grim. And even easy-going Vic seemed troubled.

Turning towards her, Rupert held out an imperative hand, closing it round her small cold fingers almost brutally.

'Sounds like there's a nuisance in the air, darling.'

'A nuisance?' Cressida looked from one to the other, a frown between her brows. 'What sort of nuisance?'

'Well, now, I don't rightly know,' said Vic in a perturbed voice. 'We had a couple of men round this morning, Rose and me. Never seen them before. Asking about people in the village.'

Unseen, Rupert's hand tightened on hers.

Cressida's eyes narrowed. 'About me, you mean?'

Vic nodded. 'I reckon so. And his lordship too.'

Cressida and Rupert exchanged glances. She had introduced him to Vic as plain Rupert Dearham and up to now Vic had called him by his Christian name.

Rupert said in a still voice, 'What did they ask about me?'

Vic shifted uncomfortably. 'Seemed to think you were staying here at the cottage with Cressida. Positive of it they were. I said to them, I said, "If you know that, it's more'n I do." And then Rose sent them off about their business.'

'Hell,' said Rupert, running his hand through his hair

n an uncharacteristic gesture. Cressida thought she had
never seen him look so agitated. 'When did they leave
you, Vic?'

The older man deliberated. ''Bout an hour or so, I'd
say. Mebbe a bit more.'

'They haven't turned up here,' Cressida mused.

'No. That means they've gone off snooping round the
village,' deduced Rupert.

Cressida's frown deepened. 'But if they're some
detectives or something of Keith's, why should they? I
mean, once they know where I live, why don't they just
tell him and be done with it?' she asked Rupert,
oblivious of Vic's embarrassed interest.

The green eyes narrowed. 'Why indeed? Perhaps we
should go and look for them and ask.'

'They were asking after the nearest public telephone,'
Vic volunteered. 'I told them, the police station,' he
added with obvious satisfaction.

Rupert gave a crack of laughter. 'I bet they didn't
like that.'

'No,' agreed Vic stolidly. 'Didn't look as if they did. I
told them there wasn't one in the pub in the village but
there was one of them noisy booth things at the place
on the crossroads, the Red Lion, I think it is.'

Rupert watched him, fascinated. 'And is there?'

'Oh yes. They've got a public phone *there*,' agreed
Vic. He thought for a couple of moments and then
added. 'Permanently vandalised it is. Never works.'

Rupert broke into a shout of laughter as Cressida,
much moved, leaned forward and kissed Vic's weather-
beaten cheek.

'You're a champion,' she told him.

He shrugged, trying and failing to disguise the fact
that he was greatly pleased. 'Didn't like the look of
them, that's all. Now you and his lordship had better be
off, if you want to stay ahead of them.'

He nodded cheerfully, wished them good luck and

was off, whistling his dog to heel. Cressida and Rupert were left staring at each other.

Cressida said slowly, '*Do* we want to stay ahead of them?'

Rupert gave a faint smile. 'That's your decision. You know my views.'

'Stay and face them?'

'Armed with a suitable story,' he agreed.

She looked away, a faint flush rising in her cheeks 'That you—that I—that we——'

'Completely,' he nodded, mock-solemn.

Her eyes were fixed on the rippling water of the stream in the sunlight. She said, 'I know I shouldn't. It isn't fair. But—I think I am a little afraid of Keith. He used to undermine me so *easily*.' She gave Rupert a rapid, shamed look. '*Would* you?' she asked simply.

He expelled a long breath. 'That's what friends are for,' he said.

By the time Keith Harley arrived, she and Rupert were sitting by the river-bank making, at least on her side, slightly stilted conversation and finishing their mid-day picnic.

'When you stop being the feminists' answer to Paul Getty, you have a promising career ahead of you as a cook,' Rupert remarked, swallowing the last piece of quiche. 'You know, you're quite perfect,' he added with the air of a connoisseur. 'Beauty, brains *and* a pastrycook.'

Cressida gave him a preoccupied smile. Her ears, attuned now to the country sounds, had picked up a braking car in the lane.

'What's the matter?' Then Rupert heard it too and turned his head. 'Ah, I see. Or rather I hear. Enter Dr Livingstone, raging.'

Cressida swallowed. 'Keith doesn't rage,' she said in a small voice.

'Not even when he sees his woman hi-jacked by an interloper? You amaze me.'

She was too jumpy to respond to his teasing. 'I am not,' she said between her teeth, 'his woman.'

'No?' The voice was light but the suddenly unveiled eyes were burning with an intensity she had never seen before. 'Are you sure? By his reckoning? By your father's?'

'By the only one's who matters,' she hissed. 'My own.'

The garden gate creaked and then swung to with a little clang. She jumped again. The green eyes noted it mockingly. Rupert turned over a little on his side, reaching out for his sun-hat which he put on the front of his head, tipping it over his eyes.

Keith came round the side of the house with the brisk, businesslike step that Cressida remembered so well. Her heart turned into a tight little ball of ice. Keith saw them and came across the grass to them at once. He stopped a couple of feet away.

'Cressida,' he said in that flat, compelling tone she also remembered. He did not spare the lounging Rupert a glance. 'Cressida, come here.'

'*Not* Dr Livingstone,' murmured Rupert wickedly. 'Young Lochinvar perhaps.' He leaned back on his elbow, looking up at Keith. 'Lochinvar in rimless spectacles,' he said in a dreamy tone.

Keith did not deign to acknowledge this sally. Nevertheless, to Cressida's amazement, a slight tinge of pink appeared about his ears.

'Cressida, I am not here to argue with you.'

'A man of peace,' intoned Rupert in his self-appointed role as Chorus.

Keith shot him a look of dislike and came a hasty step closer.

'Cressida, we have to talk. Will you ask your friend to leave us,' he said in exasperation.

Cressida found her voice. She had, after all, grown up
a lot since she last saw Keith, and her powers of
decision-making, though they stood her in no stead at
all with Lord Dearham, were, she found, quite easily
brought into play against her ex-husband.

She did not move from where she sat, lifting her chin
to look at him.

'No and no,' she said crisply.

Oddly, this did not appear to antagonise Keith. He
almost relaxed, as if this was what he was expecting and
could deal with quite easily.

'Now don't be temperamental, darling,' he said,
faintly indulgent. 'I haven't got the time.'

Cressida gave a low laugh. 'If you're short of time,
Keith, you shouldn't waste a minute on coming to see
me.'

'Of course I had to see you, darling.' The patience
was clear in his voice. 'This isn't the sort of thing that
can be discussed through lawyers. Or,' he added with a
long look at Rupert, 'in the presence of third parties.'

'We have nothing to discuss, Keith,' Cressida said
levelly.

He brushed that aside. He still had the same
magnificent assurance, she noted, that ability to ignore
what she had said as if she had not spoken at all. She
was a commodity to him, just as she always had been,
not a woman with an independent voice. She stood up,
shaking with anger.

'Look, Keith. I don't know why you're here. Though
I can guess. And it's not going to work. I got you out of
my hair six years ago and have thanked God for it
every morning since then.'

He gave a sad, whimsical smile. 'Poor child,' he said.
'I was so young, then. I never realised how much I hurt
you.'

'Not that young,' said Cressida coldly.

'Not in years maybe but I was so immature. I had put

all my life into my work.' He took an impetuous step forward, his hand out in a gesture that would have looked, to the indifferent observer, boyishly appealing. Cressida was not an indifferent observer. Her lip curled in distaste as she looked at the offered hand.

'You did indeed,' she said with irony. 'You even married it. You're mature enough to know better these days, I gather?'

Even Keith Harley's vanity was not so great as to be immune to the contempt in her voice. He fell back, pulling fussily at the tailored waistcoat of his three-piece grey linen suit.

'You should never have left me,' he muttered. 'You've changed.'

'You mean I'm not such a pushover as I used to be?' Cressida asked in a deceptively mild voice. Her eyes flashed. 'Hell's teeth, you've got a cheek, swanning in here and expecting to go back on my domestic payroll.'

He was stung. Lifting his chin he glared at her.

'I mean you've changed for the worse. Jerome told me you had. I was sorry for him. He had tears in his eyes when he told me what you had become.'

Cressida whitened. His voice was vitriolic and his careful, patronising smile had dissolved into a grimace. He was looking at her with undisguised enmity.

'That's the only reason I'm here,' Keith shrilled at her. 'Jerome begged me.'

'Then you've discharged your duty,' Cressida said very quietly. 'Please go.'

He seemed not to have heard her. 'He didn't tell me you were reduced to paying your men though,' Keith said with a vengeful titter. 'Where did you find this gigolo? Isn't he a mite expensive? And do you know he's been bragging round London that he'll get the Sebastian heiress to marry him?'

Cressida felt as if he had branded her, as if every one of his horridly familiar accusations were white-hot and laid against her skin to mark her for ever. Her eyes were dark with shock.

Suddenly, Keith Harley did not quite know how, he found himself not looking into tortured brown eyes but green ones; cool, laughing green ones that were inexplicably unnerving.

'I think you will apologise for that,' Rupert Dearham said reflectively.

'Apologise? To *you*?' echoed Keith in disbelief.

'No. To Cressida.'

The other man snorted. 'She's my wife.'

'Ex-wife,' Rupert corrected gently. 'Grossly insulted ex-wife, to be precise.'

Keith found to his utter amazement that his right arm had been taken in an easy grip and was now being forced cruelly high behind his back. He struggled and was astonished to find that his assailant seemed quite unmoved.

'I warn you,' said Keith panting, 'I am trained in karate.'

Rupert looked interested. 'Really?' The arm was pushed even higher and Keith squirmed. 'What a wonderful thing education is.' He shook him a little. He was not, Keith saw, even breathing hard. 'Now say sorry, like a good boy, and then I can stop wasting good sunbathing time like this.'

Keith glared into the handsome, amused face and read implacability there.

'All right. All right,' he said, thinking that at least there were no witnesses to tell Jerome how badly he had handled this. 'I apologise, Cressida,' he said between his teeth.

'Not very gracious,' observed Rupert. 'But then it was your first time, I take it?' He gave the writhing man a sweet smile. 'We have to make allowances for novices, darling,' he said to Cressida.

She nodded, still very white. She did not seem able to

speak.

'Good,' said Rupert. 'I'll just set him on his way then and we can go back to our—er—picnic.' He gave her a long look, full of remembered sensuality and shared amusement. Cressida did not respond but Keith, seeing it, went suddenly still. Here was a problem he had not expected. He allowed himself to be led away along the stream-side path. Rupert's grip was no longer painful but Keith was not making the mistake of struggling against it.

They came round the side of the cottage, out of sight of Cressida, and Rupert pushed him ahead of him.

'Don't come here again,' he said mildly.

Keith turned to glare at him. 'Are you threatening me, you English dummy?'

For a moment Rupert looked surprised, then really amused. Then he shook his head.

'No. Threats are more your style than mine, Mr Harley. If I want to do something, I do it. It gives me,' he explained innocently 'more satisfaction that way.'

Keith began to feel uneasy. He did not know why. The Englishman did not appear to be angry. He was talking quietly. He had no weapon. Yet Keith began to back away.

'I was merely suggesting that you don't come again. You see, I don't think Cressida likes it. And I——' he gave Keith a wide, frank smile, 'only like what Cressida likes.'

Keith's face contorted. 'Gigolo,' he spat.

'You didn't apologise to me inadvertently, did you, Mr Harley?' Rupert's voice was meditative. 'I do hope not. I would hate to be ungracious.'

And with a smooth, relaxed movement he tipped the unsuspecting Keith backwards into the fast-running stream. There was a splash, a muffled curse, an exclamation of disgust and Keith Harley stumbled, dripping, to the bank. Rupert watched him impassively.

He neither moved to help him out nor, as Keith had half-feared, to push him back in again.

Swearing, Keith floundered out, squeezing the water from the skirts of his well-cut jacket. His glasses had been knocked sideways. He adjusted them angrily, found they were misted and tried unavailingly to clear them by polishing them on a sopping handkerchief.

His dignity was now in tatters. He could never recall being outfaced like this. He was shamed and furious; furious with Rupert, with Jerome but most of all with Cressida. His mouth thinned as he thought of Cressida sitting round the corner out of sight while her bully-boy assaulted the man who, as her former husband, had every right to her respect. He bared his teeth in a caricature of a smile.

'You'll regret this, dummy.'

Rupert smiled infuriatingly. 'Oh, I don't think so. Rather the reverse, if anything. One to tell the children at bedtime. Tell us about the time you threw the nasty man in the river, Daddy, that sort of thing. They will probably,' he concluded with a touch of complacency, 'make a hero out of me for it. Though anyone,' cool, contemptuous eyes flicked Keith up and down and steel entered the light voice, '*anyone* would have done the same.'

Keith was almost beside himself with rage. 'You leave her alone,' he almost shouted. 'You hear me, dummy? You leave her alone. She's mine. She always will be. I was the first and I know her. There'll never be another man for her.'

Rupert's lip curled. For an instant the green eyes were neither cool nor laughing. Suddenly the handsome face took on an altogether different and more formidable aspect, spare and fierce. Keith's ranting died away.

Then, just as suddenly, the expression changed again and Rupert was once more smiling lazily, though not at all warmly, at his antagonist.

'Oh, I hope you're wrong,' he said. 'For both our sakes.'

And, quite as if Keith was negligible and he could not be bothered to waste any more time on him, Rupert Dearham turned his back on that rising young executive and walked back thoughtfully to the girl.

CHAPTER SEVEN

CRESSIDA was standing, taut and still, where he had left her. Under the summer tan she was very pale. The brown eyes had a queer fixed look.

Rupert said in faint amusement, 'I take it you heard the splash?'

She swallowed. 'I—yes.'

'Don't look so worried. I didn't drown him. Just gave him every reason to go away and change his clothes. So he won't be back to annoy you for a good few hours. I would guess.'

She sat down abruptly, limp as a rag doll.

'I suppose I should thank you.'

'Not at all.' He was still amused. 'I enjoyed it. Somebody should have thrown him in a river years ago. Preferably several times.'

'No, I mean for being here.' She swallowed again, not looking at him. 'I hadn't realised . . . that is, it had not occurred to me that people would think . . .'

He raised elegant brows. 'I am at a loss.'

Her head dipped, so that her expression was hidden from him. 'I'm sorry Keith called you a gigolo,' she said baldly.

'Oh.' For a moment Rupert contemplated the bent copper head in silence. Then he gave a soft laugh. 'Don't let it worry you.'

She raised her head at that, startled. Was he pretending? The green eyes were alive with laughter; he looked relaxed and slightly pleased with himself. No, he was not pretending. Cressida shook her head, trying to clear it.

'You don't mind being insulted?' she asked slowly.

Rupert looked wry. He dropped down beside her lightly on the grass.

'Does that lower me beneath contempt in your estimation?'

'Oh *no*!' Her reply was too quick and fervent to be disbelieved. 'Only . . .'

'Yes?'

'I would have expected you to be very angry,' Cressida told him honestly. 'In your position, Keith would—oh, I don't know—probably have sued for defamation of character or something. And my father——' her face was very sober '—my father would have broken him.'

Rupert smiled. 'Yes, I've heard that your father has some rather mediaeval ideas about justice. He's a vengeful man, isn't he?'

Cressida said painfully, 'He never leaves a debt unpaid. Of any sort. He's proud of it.'

Rupert reached out and ran his fingers over the back of her clasped hands. It was a comforting gesture. It was also amazingly intimate. Cressida jumped and faint colour rose in her cheeks.

'Yes, I can see why you thought I should stamp after Keith and break every bone in his body,' Rupert mused, watching the expression in her face with an unreadable smile. He began to stroke her hands in a gentle rhythm. 'It's not my style, though. Sorry to disappoint you.'

She looked down at the long, sensitive fingers that were touching her so gently. A smile dawned.

'Not exactly disappoint,' she demurred, and, looking up suddenly, she met his eyes full on. 'If you'd broken every bone in his body, it would have been a terrible nuisance to get rid of him,' she pointed out.

Rupert's firm lips quivered but he stayed commendably straight-faced. 'Just what I thought myself,' he agreed.

Cressida's hands moved, turned palm upwards, caught and held his stroking fingers.

'Thank you,' she said simply.

He looked down at their clasped hands with an odd smile curling his mouth. He hesitated visibly and Cressida tensed. But in the end, all he said was, 'Forget it. A privilege of friendship.'

It was impossible to forget, though, as became gradually apparent throughout the rest of the day. Their easy comradeship had been dispelled by Keith's intrusion. Their conversation became stilted. Cressida found herself falling silent mid-sentence, as she watched Rupert's face anxiously for his reactions. She did not want to be but she was in full retreat. Almost in despair she recognised her old characteristics welling up to take charge of her: shyness, restraint, guarded responses.

And Rupert recognised it too. At last he said, 'You know, I have the feeling you'd rather be left on your own.'

Cressida protested but without conviction. He paid no attention.

'You don't have to lie to be polite,' he said with the first signs of irritation she had ever received from him. 'And you have every right to ask me to leave. I'd probably do the same in your place.'

Cressida blushed, mumbling something unintelligible about needing to work. His eyes narrowed.

'Does that mean you are going back to town?'

She nodded. 'During the day.'

There was a pause. 'What do you mean?' Rupert asked softly, a hint of anger licking under the smooth voice.

'Why, only that I don't stay in the flat,' said Cressida, bewildered at the smoky fury in his eyes. She frowned, puzzled. 'I don't like it, you see. I only stay there when I have to. It's not my home. I commute up from here normally. I leave my car at the station and go up to Paddington.'

Rupert relaxed. 'I see.'

'What did you think I meant?' she asked, with some daring.

He gave her a swift, brooding look. 'I thought you were warning me off.' And as she continued to stare at him in incomprehension, he added mockingly, 'Along the lines of "but don't bother to follow me because I won't be available to see you in the evenings!"'

She was shocked. 'I wouldn't do that.'

Rupert continued to look searchingly into her eyes. Then he shrugged.

'Really, I wouldn't,' she insisted. 'I wouldn't want to, anyway. I thought we were friends now. Don't friends see each other in the evenings?'

'Right,' he said, as if he were throwing down a challenge, 'when?'

She came back at once. 'Whenever you say.'

He looked past her. 'Tomorrow then,' he said flatly. 'Here at eight. I'll take you out to dinner.'

She said half to herself, 'There'll be a lot to catch up on tomorrow. I don't know . . .'

Rupert took her by the shoulders and spun her round to face him. The handsome face was grim.

'If you don't want to see me again, you only have to say so. Don't *lie* to me with excuses about work.'

She stood very still between his hands, her heart hammering. She felt oddly exhilarated by his harshness, though she did not understand why. She stayed cool, however.

'I was thinking,' she remarked, 'that as there will be a lot of work to do, if I am to be here washed and brushed up by eight o'clock, I shall have to leave earlier than usual in the morning. That's all.'

There was a momentary silence, while their eyes locked. Then Rupert's hands fell away and he began to laugh. She raised an eyebrow in query but he shook his head, still laughing.

'God help me, I'd forgotten you were a conscientious executive.'

'There is something wrong with that?' she asked frostily, relieved that the tension was dissipated but offended by his mockery.

'Oh no. Nothing at all, it's very commendable. I'm just not used to it.' He grinned down at her. 'And you don't look very executive at the moment.'

In illustration of his remark, he fluffed up her loose hair round her face. Cressida gave a little shiver. She was finding that whenever he touched her—particularly when it was in one of these casual gestures without passion or intent—she felt a surge of warmth through her like an electric current. It was very disturbing, particularly as she was not sure whether he knew it or not. Sometimes there was something in his eyes which made her think that he was aware of every flickering response and of her alarm at her own feelings. Sometimes she thought he was completely oblivious.

She stepped away from his hands. 'For that matter you don't look like a successful entrepreneur either, just at this moment,' she said, eyeing his sun-hat eloquently.

Rupert laughed. 'Ah, but I'm only a successful entrepreneur by chance. It sort of crept up on me when I wasn't looking. I'm really an amateur explorer, a boffin, a botanist, a disorganised eccentric. And that's what I look like.'

Cressida said with irony, 'I wouldn't say you were disorganised. You seem pretty effective to me.'

'Do I?' He sounded almost sad.

She was curious. 'Don't you want to be effective?'

He gave her his lopsided smile, full of self-mockery. 'You mean don't I want to have my own way? Well, of course the answer to that has to be yes. Everyone wants his own way, I imagine. But some people want it at no matter what price.'

'Not you?' she asked into the silence that fell.

'Me?' Rupert almost jumped. She had the feeling that he had been recalled a great distance and that wherever he had been it was no happy place. 'Oh no, not me. I'm an easy-going chap. I only want what I can get at reasonable cost.'

Cressida stood very still. She knew that this was important, though she did not understand why. But there was that faint undertone of bitterness that had marred his light-hearted tones before and she was put on her guard by it.

She said carefully, 'What is an unreasonable cost, then?'

Rupert said almost with violence, 'Your whole life.' She said nothing and he went on with a return to his lighter voice, 'There are some satisfactions you can only have if you change your life entirely to fit in with them. Some women, too.'

She said very quietly, 'A woman you have wanted, Rupert?'

At first she thought he would not answer. The handsome face was shuttered, the mouth a grim slash.

Then he said in a low voice, 'A woman I still want.'

She flinched at that. It was extraordinary how much it hurt that Rupert should want another woman. Another woman? What was she thinking of? Rupert did not want her, or not in any other than a very passing way, and she did not want him to want her. She did not want any man to do so. So why did she feel as if she had been punched under the heart when he said there was a woman he wanted?

Seeing her expression, he seemed to shake himself free of his thoughts, giving her one of his wry smiles.

'A new experience for me,' he told her. 'Wanting someone I can't have. Very character-forming.'

She wondered who the woman could be, how she could resist him. The thought struck her with surprise. It was a long time since she had thought of a man in that way; and she had never found one irresistible. Cressida avoided his eyes, wondering worriedly whether the glamorous Lord Dearham could possibly be about to become the first man she had fallen hopelessly in love with in the whole of her well-ordered life.

'It must be,' she said with an effort. 'You have my sympathy.'

'Have I?' His voice was dry. 'Well, that's better than nothing, I suppose.' He extracted his car keys from his jacket pocket and surveyed them, faintly frowning. 'I'll see you tomorrow night. Don't be late or I shall stand outside your house and bay like a hungry wolf until you let me in.'

Cressida laughed; it was a less constrained sound but she was still tense. She was glad that he made no attempt to kiss her before he left, but oddly disappointed too.

You are going bats, she told herself severely in the hall mirror as the sound of his car's engine died away. Either you want him to kiss you or you don't. You can't want both at the same time. And yet—in spite of that relief—she was conscious of a deep and inexplicable dissatisfaction.

'*Damn!*' she said, in an explosion of unusual temper and flung herself into ruthless tidying of the kitchen.

The next day, in her office, nobody would have recognised the tempestuous house-cleaner in cool Mrs Harley. Cressida caught sight of herself in the mirrored entrance hall and contrasted the composed image with that which had confronted her from yesterday's mirror. How completely the image had changed. And how very little different she felt inside.

She went slowly to her office. What was it that had happened to her? Why, after only a few days of Rupert Dearham's company, did she feel so changed? It was like being young and breathless and uncertain again; and hopeful. Oh yes, thought Cressida, a little grimly, she had not felt so alive and hopeful for years, if ever. And there was absolutely no reason for it. She sat behind her desk and put her hands flat on the fresh blotter. No reason at all, she told herself firmly, all too aware of the warmth inside her.

The door to her secretary's room opened and Lesley Button came in.

'Hello,' she said. 'You look happy. Bought a gold mine?'

Cressida grinned. If she told Lesley Button that she was sitting here smiling to herself for no better reason than because she was thinking of Rupert Dearham, Lesley would think she was mad. It tempted her. She put her head on one side.

'Not bought, exactly.' Cressida demurred. 'Maybe gambled on one.'

Lesley's eyes narrowed but all she said was, 'Well, you're looking good on it, anyway.'

'So far,' agreed Cressida, with a return of the doubts that could never be long suppressed. She shrugged. For today, at least, she could put them out of her head. She had plenty of work to do. She need not think of Rupert Dearham until five to eight tonight. 'Have you typed up the Fellini contract?' she asked briskly.

Lesley raised the file in her hand. 'Here.'

'Copies gone to the lawyers?'

'Theirs and ours, yes.' She put the folder down on Cressida's desk. 'And everything you sent in over the last few days has been typed and circulated.'

Cressida smiled. 'Thank God for computer links,' she said, referring to the small work-station that had been installed at the cottage. 'And for brilliant secretaries.'

Lesley dipped her head graciously. 'I aim to give satisfaction.' She hesitated, as if in two minds about what she was going to say next, and then went on in a rush, 'I didn't have anything through on the Queen

Anne's Place project, though. Michael has been hopping in and out of the office every day wanting to know whether you had read his report.'

Cressida stared at her secretary, her heart sinking. How had she thought she could put Rupert Dearham out of her mind for five minutes, let alone a working day?

Misinterpreting her expression, Lesley explained, 'The company Mr Sebastian wants to buy from Lord Dearham's group.'

'Yes,' said Cressida. It sounded hollow.

Lesley looked puzzled. 'Yes, you've read the report, or yes, you know which company?'

'Both,' said Cressida heavily.

Lesley looked a little alarmed. 'Do you mean that you wrote a note to Michael and I've lost it off the computer? I've never done a thing like that before. When did you send it?'

Cressida halted her with one raised finger. 'No note,' she said. 'You haven't lost it.'

Lesley stared. Cressida's smile was lopsided.

'It's not a thing it would be tactful to put on to paper. I will speak to Michael. And,' she added, with the slightest hint of squared shoulders, 'to my father.'

'Ah,' said Lesley, instantly comprehending. 'So Michael was right. Mr Sebastian won't be pleased.'

'You,' said Cressida, picking up the folder in front of her, 'are so right. Mr Sebastian is not going to be pleased with me at all, today.'

And when her father's telephone call was put through to her at half past twelve, Cressida's fears were fully realised.

'Hello, Papa,' she said equably. 'You're up early.'

He snorted down the telephone in frustrated anger. 'With a daughter like you, it's a wonder I can get to bed at all, much less sleep. What the hell do you think you're doing?'

Cressida glanced at the illuminated display screen on

her desk which showed her timetable for the next month.

'Fellini this afternoon and probably most of tomorrow,' she reported. 'Preparation for the marketing conference in Paris, Finance Director's Report . . .'

She was cut off by an outraged bellow. 'I don't want to know what's in your bloody diary. I want to know what you've been saying to Keith.'

Cressida whitened but she did not lose her self-possession. Her father was a great deal easier to deal with by transatlantic telephone than in person. She still hated the loud voice and the abuse, of course. Dispassionately she watched the way her hand had clenched round the handset so that her knuckles stood out white. No, she had not got any more able to deal with those volcanic tantrums. On the other hand, when Jerome could not see the effect that his raging was having on her, she felt she could maintain some pretence of calm.

So, 'Saying to Keith?' she echoed in a cool voice. 'Not a lot.'

'I don't need you to tell me that!' Jerome roared.

'Oh, Keith has already reported in, has he?' she asked with irony.

Jerome gave no indication of having heard the remark. 'Do you realise he is in England especially to talk to you? Have you any idea what that is costing?'

'Him or you?' she asked dulcetly.

But Jerome was quite shameless. 'The company, of course. We can't afford to have senior executives away from their desks for weeks on end while they dance attendance on my daughter.'

'So recall him,' Cressida said without emotion.

Even Jerome could not fail to hear that. He switched his tone instantly.

'Look, Cress, why don't you give the boy a chance? He knows he's made a mistake.'

Cressida thought of Keith's bland conceit, the arrogance of his approach to her at the cottage. 'He does indeed,' she agreed.

'Then why . . .?'

'Look,' Cressida said suddenly, interrupting in her turn, 'we've had this conversation before. I don't want to have anything to do with Keith. And that's final. I'll have my lawyer write him a letter if you like. Maybe you should have one too. No more Keith. I don't want to hear his name again. Do I make myself clear?'

There was a silence at the other end not wholly attributable to transatlantic delay on the line.

Then Jerome said, 'Keith says you've got yourself a boyfriend.' His tone said plainly that he thought Keith was hallucinating.

'Does he?' said Cressida uncommunicatively.

'Now Cress, you're not doing anything silly, are you?'

Damn him, she thought, he sounded concerned. The hectoring had stopped and now he sounded like any normal parent, loving and full of protective anxiety. She hardened her heart. She knew how quickly he would revert to type if she showed any sign of responding to this sign of affection. Rupert was right. All Jerome wanted was total domination.

She said coolly, 'I'm enjoying myself.'

It was, of course, a deliberately provocative remark. Jerome's voice sharpened, the cloak of anxious father slipping somewhat.

'Keith tells me you're making a fool of yourself over that good-for-nothing Rupert Dearham.'

Cressida was surprised how angry she was. For a moment she could not speak with it. The urge to defend Rupert—and attack Keith—was almost overwhelming. Almost.

One of Cressida's greatest strengths as an executive, however, was her ability not to allow herself to be side-tracked. Deciding, reluctantly, that her father's opinion of Lord Dearham was a minor issue, she calmed herself.

'You told me to get to know him,' she reminded Jerome therefore, in her most reasonable tone of voice. 'In fact, if you remember, you told me to go to bed with him.' She paused and added ironically, 'For the good of the company, of course.'

There was a strangled sound from the telephone.

'Do you want to change your instructions?' Cressida asked, enjoying herself.

Jerome said in a whisper, 'Are you sleeping with Rupert Dearham?'

'Whether I am or not, it is none of your business,' Cressida told him evenly, 'since I am *not* doing it on instructions. What is more, I have read Michael's report on the take-over project and it is quite clear you just want that company for its property. You will close down that business—which is perfectly profitable—and throw all those people out of work just because you want the building they work in. There are times, Papa, when you make it very hard for people to defend you.'

'It's a lie,' said Jerome at once, going on to the attack as she had seen him do so often at uncomfortable enquiries from the press or the opposition's lawyers. 'I've negotiated in good faith. What has Dearham been telling you?'

'Not a thing,' said Cressida wearily. 'It's all in Michael's report. The conclusions are obvious.'

'Report? What report? I authorised no report. Collect all the copies and destroy them immediately.' Jerome's voice cracked down the line like a whip. 'If it got out, it could be dynamite. How could you let him do it, Cress? Are you stupid or something?'

'If listening to the advice I get from the people who are paid to advise me makes me stupid, then I suppose I am,' she retorted. 'Michael——'

He cut her off. 'I never should have trusted that guy. I never should have trusted you. There's only one person in this company that's loyal to me and that's the man you're happy to ditch for a phony playboy.'

The injustice of this was so great that, in spite of her distress, Cressida could not prevent a laugh. It was a sharp, tense bark of sound and it infuriated her father.

'Can you deny it? Can you deny it?' he shouted at her.

'Oh, come on, Papa. The only ditching that has been done was by Keith. Of me. Long before the divorce. What I do with my life now is nothing to do with him. Or you.'

'You'll regret it,' Jerome warned bitterly. 'He's on his beam ends. He's only after your money.'

The flame of anger burned up again, brighter and fiercer. How dared he talk like that about Rupert? How *dared* he? But Cressida did not lose her cool.

'Keith?' she asked innocently.

There was another silence. Then Jerome said with grim dignity, 'Since you're obviously determined to be childish, I won't waste my time any longer. But if you're fool enough to get involved with Rupert Dearham, don't come crying to me if he takes your money and leaves you flat. It will only be what you deserve.'

He slammed the telephone down without waiting for her reply. Cressida replaced the instrument in its cradle more slowly. She had stood up to him pretty well, she thought, but the conversation had left her shaken.

Lesley put her head round the door. 'Coffee?'

Cressida nodded in gratitude. Lesley disappeared and then returned with a steaming mug.

'Problems?' she asked.

Cressida shrugged. 'When aren't there?' She sipped her coffee, grateful for the warmth.

Lesley watched her shrewdly.

'Mr Harley rang twice this morning,' she said without

expression. 'I told him you were busy. He said he'd call again.'

Cressida swirled the coffee round and round in her mug, staring at it absorbedly.

'And has he?'

'Not yet. I told him I didn't know when you'd be free.' Lesley's voice was carefully neutral. 'He intends to invite you out to dinner this evening. I told him,' there was a faint query in her voice, 'that I did not keep your private diary so I did not know whether you would be available.'

This was the strict truth. Nevertheless, since so many of Cressida's professional engagements took place in the evening, she usually gave Lesley a list of her private arrangements, to avoid double-booking or Lesley's having to check with her on each occasion. The diary would, of course, show nothing for this evening.

There was no reason for the faint blush that rose in Cressida's cheeks. Lesley noticed it with interest and some surprise.

'I'm already going out to dinner tonight,' Cressida said with a fair attempt at nonchalance. 'I forgot to tell you.'

Lesley nodded, making a note on her pad. 'Shall I tell Mr Harley when he rings?'

Cressida was tempted. But no, it would be cowardly, and anyway was not the sort of thing that it was proper to ask a secretary to do, however good a friend she might be.

'No, it's all right. I'll take my own medicine,' she said. 'Put him through when he rings.'

But Keith Harley, perhaps discouraged by Lesley's manner or Cressida's previous unavailability, did not call back. When Cressida closed her safe with a clang and dialled the combination, it was to news from Lesley that there had been no further personal calls for Cressida.

'Good.' Cressida slipped on the jacket of her suit and went to the mirror, straightening the lapels slightly, moving her shoulders inside its tailored perfection until it sat absolutely right. Lesley watched her, smiling.

'Going out straight from work?'

Cressida shook her head.

'Oh, you're off to the flat then?'

Again the negative. Cressida looked mischievous.

'I'm going out for a bucolic evening's entertainment in the country.'

Lesley chuckled. 'If your father knew you'd taken to maypole dancing, he'd be over here like a shot.'

Cressida gave a little shiver. It was a little too near the truth. She did not really believe that Jerome Sebastian would abandon his imminent deals to fly into London on the trail of an erring daughter, but there was always that faint possibility. It made Cressida turn cold to think of it.

'Don't say such things,' she said to Lesley. 'Not even as a joke.'

'Right,' said Lesley with ready understanding. 'So tell me instead where you're doing this maypole dancing.'

'I don't know,' Cressida confessed. 'I've left the details to my—er—companion.'

'Companion?' Lesley's brows rose. She pursed her lips in a silent and unladylike whistle. 'Not just rural pursuits but a rustic swain as well. You *are* living dangerously.'

Cressida sent another, surreptitious look at her image in the mirror. In spite of the sober suit and neat, businesslike hair-style, she did not look her normal, composed self. There was faint colour in her cheeks and, surely, her eyes were not usually as bright as that? She looked eager, expectant; and several centuries younger, she thought wryly.

'Dangerously is the word,' she agreed. She patted her hair down into place and then, suddenly, whirled round

on Lesley and danced her across the room. 'It's terrific
fun.' She let Lesley go and spun several circles on her
own, swinging her arms out wide. The restrained hair
broke loose again and two hairpins broke free and fell
to the carpet. Cressida ignored them, hugging her arms
round herself. 'Oh, I am enjoying myself so much.'

Wordlessly Lesley retrieved the pins and held them
out to her. Cressida stuffed them in her pocket,
twinkling.

'Don't look so disapproving,' she teased. 'It's only a
silly old maypole dance after all.'

'Is it?' said Lesley. But by that time Cressida was out
of the door and halfway down the hall, humming, and
did not hear her.

CHAPTER EIGHT

WHEN Rupert arrived, Cressida was not ready. This was not because she had been late home. On the contrary, she had caught an earlier train home than usual and had found a seat with several minutes to spare, in contrast to her usual last-minute dash. Nor had the car given her any difficulty. She had made the journey home in record time.

The trouble started when she tried to decide what to wear. He had not said where they were going. Rupert was, however, sufficiently sophisticated to make it clear if he was taking her to a full-scale ball. Therefore she could rule out a long dress and diamonds. That, however, left her with an almost infinite number of permutations.

Cressida, who did not like clothes and spent the minimum of time deciding what she would wear for an ordinary evening out, ran through practically her entire wardrobe, pulling clothes out, trying them on, discarding them, trying them on again. By the time Rupert rang the bell, her normally tidy bedroom looked like a vast jumble sale and she was still wearing her robe, with her hair pinned up on top of her head from her shower.

She opened the door to him shamefacedly. Seeing her, just for a moment his eyes flared and narrowed. And then, like the blink of a camera lens, it was gone and he was leaning one hand against the door jamb and laughing down at her.

'Don't tell me,' he said. 'Let me guess. You find you haven't got a thing to wear.'

Cressida flushed and opened the door to let him in, a little huffily.

'Well, I don't know where we're supposed to be going,' she defended herself. 'Or what you expect.'

He followed her into the hall, redolent of the scent of roses from a bowl on the window ledge.

'Would my expectations make any difference?' Rupert asked curiously.

Cressida was leading the way into the tiny sitting-room but at that she turned and looked back at him over her shoulder in surprise.

'Of course.'

Rupert looked at her for a long moment, his eyes warm, but all he said was, 'How very unliberated.'

Cressida put up a distracted hand to her descending hair and said calmly, 'Don't be banal. Where *are* we going tonight?'

Rupert's lips twitched. 'I thought you'd probably seen enough up-market restaurants to last you a lifetime in your professional existence.'

Cressida smiled. 'Shrewd of you.'

'Yes.' He allowed himself to assume a ridiculously complacent expression. 'So I thought you'd rather go somewhere—er—quieter.'

'It sounds as if we're going to a transport café on the motorway,' she said with resignation. 'And I was thinking of wearing Ungaro!' She gave him a mocking look. 'How glad I am that I did not get dressed before you arrived.'

She turned to offer him a drink while she finished getting ready, to find that he was surveying her with that mischievous appreciation with which she was becoming familiar. The words died on her lips. She forgot about the drink, or indeed anything else, as he reached for her.

'So,' said Rupert, his eyes gleaming, 'am I.'

His hands slid under the loose robe. Cressida felt herself drawn towards him, without thought of resistance or protest. His long fingers were cool against her skin.

She murmured his name, hardly recognising her own voice in the husky desirous tone. He bent his head and feathered the lightest of kisses across her bottom lip while his hands moved surely on her body. She swayed forward, dazed by the surge of unfamiliar feeling, and his arms tightened. The next kiss was not so playful.

Her hands were trapped against the hard wall of his chest. Under her fingers she could feel the steady rhythm of his heart. It disconcerted her. She pushed herself a little away from him, shaking her head as if to dispel a mist from her eyes. She looked at him uncertainly, warily. His face was still amused.

She said in a low voice, 'Rupert, I don't want . . .'

'I know what you don't want.' His voice was dry. 'Exactly. But if you also don't want to rouse the beast in me, you shouldn't dance around in silk underwear and a highly accessible dressing-gown.'

Cressida stepped back, shamefaced. Rupert's arms fell away. She scanned his face anxiously for some clue to his mood but the eyes were hidden under steep, down-dropped lids and his mouth was smiling.

She said in a low voice, 'I'm sorry. I didn't think. I never meant to—to *tease*.' The last word came out on an explosion of distress.

'No. I know that too.' Rupert said. 'Be thankful I do.'

She fumbled with the loosened sash of her robe, drawing it tightly round her body and knotting it with quick, savage movements. She did not look at him.

'I'm sorry,' she said again, stiffly.

'Forget it.' Rupert sounded quite kind but rather weary. 'It's not important.'

It was not a disclaimer that Cressida found comforting. She retreated even further, taking refuge in her social manner.

'I am being very neglectful. I should have offered you a drink at once. What would you like?'

There was a little silence. She turned away from him

to survey her stock of bottles and decanters but she could feel his eyes scorching through the fabric of her robe as if she had, at last, made him really angry.

'Whisky and soda,' he said evenly.

Cressida poured it for him, pleased to see that her hands did not shake in the task. Inside she was miserably conscious of being off balance and floundering. She brought it to him with a cool smile, though she could not meet his eyes. Her glance slid past him to alight on the bookshelf behind his head.

'Ice?' she asked a fine edition of Dryden's poetry.

'I'll get it. You finish dressing.'

She surrendered the glass into his hands carefully so that their fingers did not touch. Her heart lurched as he took it from her. Then she took a pace back.

'Very well. But what am I supposed to be wearing?'

Rupert shrugged, though his eyes, she found, were uncomfortably intent. 'Whatever you usually wear for dining at home.'

At that she was so startled that she forgot to avoid his eyes.

'At home? *Here?* But I've nothing in.'

'*My* home,' he explained gently.

'Your——?' Cressida was completely nonplussed. 'But I thought you lived in London. That is, I assumed . . .'

Rupert smiled at her pleasantly. 'The trouble with you, Cressida, is that you assume altogether too much. Why didn't you ask me? I kept waiting for you to ask where I was staying when I left you and you never did.'

'I didn't want to intrude,' Cressida said, bewildered by the irritation in his voice and faintly offended. 'After all, it was your own affair. It had nothing to do with me.'

'Ah!' He sipped his drink watching her. 'That's the nub, isn't it? My affairs have nothing to do with you. And that's the way you want it to stay.'

'That's the way it *is*,' she pointed out.

He put his glass down. 'But,' Rupert said very softly, 'that could change.'

She was still assimilating this when he seized hold of her shoulders, shaking her faintly.

'What am I going to do with you?' Rupert sounded rueful but to Cressida's ears there was a note of real pain there as well.

She was puzzled and let him see it. He gave a half-laughing groan, his hands tightening on her shoulders.

'Why are you so locked away? Why don't you *see* . . .? Oh hell, what have I got to lose?' Rupert exclaimed.

And he dragged her hard into his arms. This time she was not prepared and her lips opened in a gasp of shock. At once her mouth was invaded, while his hands went up to clasp the back of he head, not permitting her to evade him.

Alarm shot through her. She had never been kissed like this before, never tasted naked hunger in a man's mouth and felt an answering hunger begin to rise in herself. Cressida felt her heart give one gigantic somersault, as if she were in a falling elevator. She clutched his arms convulsively, as wave on wave of panic and something that was darker and deeper than panic washed over her.

Rupert's hold changed. He was no longer clasping her head, clamping her against him as if she might seek to escape. In one sense he was not holding her at all, for his hands were moving over her body lightly, caressing the line of bone, savouring every curve and angle. As he moved his thumb sensuously up and down a shoulder blade, Cressida shivered, her mouth suddenly dry. He slid his hand, warm palm against the skin of her back, under the fragile shoulder strap of her camisole and slipped it off. It was only then that Cressida realised that she was standing in a pool of her own robe. It had fallen unnoticed in their mutual absorption.

Rupert raised his head and looked down at her. Cressida returned his look gravely. She was dimly aware that the camisole had fallen to her hips, that her hair had abandoned its pins and that her breath was coming rather fast. Rupert slid both hands up her neck and under her hair, fanning it out over his fingers along her shoulders. Cressida stood very still.

She did not know what she wanted. She felt too many conflicting emotions tumbling in her head. She recognised that she was frightened—frightened as any schoolgirl—at this intimation of passion. She was also aware of a new and punishing need, almost a physical pain, she had never even imagined before. Above all, more insistent than either the fear or the longing, was a desperate concern for Rupert. He was her friend. He was a kind man. She must not let that kindness or offered friendship trap him. Keith had told her too often of her shortcomings for Cressida to have an illusion that she might be a pleasant lover. And if she were to fall in love with Rupert, that would be an unreasonable burden for him to bear. After all, he had a right, as any man would have, to expect that a woman of her age and experience would not cast herself wholly into his power like some neurotic adolescent.

So she stood still and quiet under his hands. At last he gave a long sigh.

'I didn't mean to do that,' Rupert said. 'It wasn't fair and I'm sorry.'

He turned away from her, picking up his drink again with a hand which, Cressida was astonished to see, was not entirely steady. She felt very cold. His rejection hurt sharply, like the point of a rapier against her quivering senses. Silently she struggled back into the camisole and drew the robe back round her shoulders.

Rupert swallowed his whisky, not looking at her.

She said in a still voice, 'I'll get dressed. If we're still going?'

'We're going,' Rupert told her expressionlessly.

She left him.

In her bedroom she scrambled into the nearest garments, hardly noticing, after all her agonising, what it was that she put on in the end. She brushed her hair with short vicious strokes but seemed completely incapable of putting it up. In the end, with an exclamation of disgust, she gave up and tied it back with a silk scarf.

When she returned, Rupert was sitting in the window-seat, responding to affectionate overtures from the smaller cat. Cressida hesitated in the doorway, fully expecting him to make some comment that her animals were less inhibited than she was.

But he merely looked up and smiled.

'Very nice,' he said. 'But bring a shawl or something. In the ancestral hall it gets a bit chilly in the evening, even in high summer.'

Cressida laughed, relieved that they had apparently returned to the plane of ordinary comradeship.

'Oh, it's a gothic pile, is it?' she teased.

Rupert's answer did not come at once. When it did, his eyes were dancing.

'I don't think many people would call it gothic, precisely,' he demurred, and, most annoyingly, refused to say any more, though he retained his look of secret amusement all the way there. Cressida could have hit him.

When they finally turned into an all-but-hidden lane and made their way over a rutted path under low-hanging trees, she gave him an ironic look.

'Not gothic? With a wood like Sleeping Beauty's Castle?'

'The wood,' he allowed, 'could do with some attention.'

And then they were out of the overhanging branches and approaching one of the most exquisite William and Mary houses Cressida had ever seen. In the summer evening it glowed with the dying radiance of the sun, warm and tranquil and welcoming.

Cressida drew a long breath. 'I didn't think houses like that existed outside the pages of historical novels,' she confessed, awed.

Rupert was pleased. But all he said was, 'Yes, it's nice, isn't it?'

'Nice? It's perfect.' She swung round in her seat, suddenly struck by a thought. 'Is your father here?'

'Dad?' For a moment he was puzzled, then he smiled. 'Oh, I see what you mean. No, Dad lives in the north in the ancient pile that goes with the title. This is a subsidiary place, used for housing unwanted wives and mad great-aunts.'

'I see.' Cressida eyed him. 'And into which category do you fall?'

Rupert stopped the car in the lee of an old brick wall and killed the engine.

'Neither,' he agreed. 'But I've always been fond of it and when my father sold it, I managed to wheel and deal somewhat and bought it back.'

'Your father *sold* it?' Cressida was shocked.

Rupert shrugged. 'A season at Cannes where he had a bad run at the tables. He's very expensive, my Dad.' He swung his long legs out of the car. 'Come and look,' he invited, clearly changing the subject.

Cressida followed him slowly, a slight frown between her brows. There was a faint edge of bitterness when he spoke of his father, in spite of the casual tone, that disturbed her. Coming up to his shoulder she slipped her hand silently into his. For a second he stiffened, then his fingers closed round her own and they walked into the house hand in hand.

The hallway was softly lit, though the sconces in the wall held electric-light bulbs rather than the candles she instinctively looked for. Following her gaze Rupert grinned.

'You're a romantic,' he teased. 'Candles leave terrible marks on the walls and ceilings. You have to redecorate at least once a year to keep the place clean.'

Cressida gave him a long look. 'You know, I'm not sure I like the way you seem to be able to read my mind,' she remarked.

Rupert squeezed the hand he was still holding. 'You've got such a transparent face.'

She laughed but grimaced. 'I hope my opponents in business don't share your view.'

The fine brows flew up. 'But I thought *I* was a business opponent,' he remarked provocatively.

Cressida refused to rise. 'Of my father's, maybe. Not mine. I haven't a single deal going with you nor you with me.'

Rupert allowed himself a small chuckle. 'Oh, I don't know. I can think of one or two—er—transactions with you that might be rewarding.'

She removed her hand, indignant at this blatant teasing. 'I hope dinner is included among them,' she told him coolly. 'I'm starving.'

'Of course.' He did not try to recapture her hand but he smiled down at her with affection. 'Come into the kitchen and let me show off.'

She followed him. 'You're cooking?' she asked, impressed.

'Don't worry, I won't poison you. In fact, I think I'm pretty good considering I'm self-taught.'

'I'm sure you are.' The odd thing was that she was sure. It suddenly occurred to her that whatever Rupert Dearham set his hand to, he would do well. She said slowly, 'You're a perfectionist, aren't you?'

He opened the door for her to precede him into the kitchen. As she did so he looked down at her thoughtfully.

'Now that's very perceptive of you. It's true. But not many people notice.'

On a note of discovery, Cressida said, 'I feel as if I know you very well. As if we've been friends all my life.'

'Do you?' He was enigmatic, neither agreeing nor denying, his expression unrevealing. 'Well, let's test my cooking and see if that comes as a horrid surprise.'

The kitchen was a warm, unmodernised apartment on the grand scale. There were two huge Welsh dressers, one at each end of the flagged stone floor, and what appeared to be a random collection of cupboards and shelves in various woods, set round the walls. A large window gave on to a square lawn, surrounded by flowering shrubs with what was clearly some kind of copse behind them. There was a wooden seat on the lawn in a patch of late sunshine. Rupert nodded at it.

'Would you like to take a drink outside while I put the soup on?'

Cressida hesitated. 'Can't I do anything?'

He shook his head decisively. 'No. I'm all planned and prepared. All you have to do is look beautiful, eat it and say thank you nicely.'

She laughed. 'Will two out of three suffice?'

'Nope.' Rupert frowned at her. 'And you're doing it again.'

'Doing what?'

'Denigrating yourself. I won't have it.' He bent and kissed her swiftly before turning to a substantial refrigerator and extracting from it an earthenware pot.

Cressida swallowed hard, shaken by the brief, casual caress. Even in the days when she and Keith were first married he had never touched her as Rupert did, with such open affection. In public Keith's gestures had been proprietorial and in private—involuntarily, Cressida shuddered remembering how it had become, in the end. There had been such hostility between them, like a pack of clear ice, so that they could see each other perfectly clearly but not approach or hear what the other one said.

They had stopped making love by then, of course. Though that had never been very satisfactory. Cressida had been too anxious, too afraid of being clumsy, and Keith had never invited confidences so she was too shy to talk about it. She thought suddenly, 'I could have talked to Rupert', and then blushed to her hair at the unbidden thought.

Fortunately Rupert was engaged in transferring the pot of soup to the Aga stove and had his back to her. She pressed her palms against her cheeks, feeling the heat in them and willing it to subside. 'What is happening to me?' she thought.

'Right. We can eat as soon as you like—or as late,' Rupert told her, straightening. 'What can I get you to drink?'

Cressida looked longingly at the splash of sun on the lawn. 'Wine?' she asked tentatively. 'Cool white wine?'

He grinned. 'You have perfect taste. It's in the fridge with the glasses. We'll take it outside.'

Seated on the ancient wooden seat, with a frosted glass of wine in her hand, Cressida sighed contentedly. Rupert looked down at her, in the act of pouring his own wine.

'Why the sigh?'

She smiled up at him, contentment in every line of her.

'Pure pleasure,' she assured him. 'I was just thinking—I'm not often as happy as I am at this moment.'

He did not smile in return. For a moment he did not respond at all, standing very still, almost as if he were holding his breath. Then he seemed to shake himself, resumed pouring the wine into his glass, and returned the bottle to its ice-filled bucket. Then he sat down. But not next to her; he sat on the grass, cross-legged.

'It doesn't take a lot to make you happy, does it?' he asked in an odd voice.

She sipped her wine. 'Doesn't it?' she teased. 'Being waited on hand and foot? My every whim anticipated? Story-book surroundings?' She gestured to indicate the little sun-filled clearing in which they sat. 'Who wouldn't be happy?'

'Lots of women I know would be bored.' Rupert suddenly raised his head and gave her a surprisingly piercing look before the lazy lids dropped and he was laughing again. 'And distinctly peeved at not being taken to dine and dance at a smart establishment.'

Cressida stretched like a cat in the evening's rays of sunlight. 'But you guessed I have too much of that sort of thing anyway,' she pointed out. 'Even if I liked it. Which I don't.'

'No,' Rupert agreed. He looked down at his glass, swirling the wine in it, so that it glinted green and lemon, like a diamond refracting light. 'What *do* you like, Cressida?'

'Sun,' she said flippantly. 'And wine. And the scent of rosemary.'

'Seriously.'

'Oh.' She sobered. 'Well, this I suppose. Being here.'

'Being here with me?' Rupert asked softly.

'Well——' Cressida was confused, bewildered, not sure what she was being asked. 'Yes. Obviously.'

'Ah!' He gave a little sigh and put down his glass, leaning back on one arm to look up at her. He looked very pleased with himself, she thought. She half expected him to reach out for her again but all he said was, 'Good!'

After that they sat and chatted like the old friends Cressida felt they were. When the sun went in, Rupert took her back into the house for a perfectly cooked meal which they ate in a little room opening out of the kitchen, watching the sunset. He did not touch her again which filled Cressida with an odd restlessness.

To disguise it she said, as he set cheese before them, 'Do

you always eat in here?'

'You mean is there no dining-room?' he interpreted, chuckling. 'And yes, of course there is. If I ever had a large party—which I don't, at least not down here—I would use it. But we open this place to the public and the dining-room is rather spectacular. So we leave it all dressed up, with the best china and glass on display, to give the tourists their money's worth.'

Cressida looked at him curiously. He sounded quite unconcerned. 'Do you mind having strangers tramping through your home?'

'Mind?' Rupert looked quite startled. 'I love it. It means I can keep the place on, at least for the time being. Houses like this are damned expensive, you know. I couldn't afford the upkeep on what I earn from the travel company. It has to pay for itself to a large extent.'

Cressida was intrigued. 'And does it?'

He shrugged. 'More or less. We're not on the main tourist circuit but enough discerning people spend a few days in Oxford and we're within striking distance of that. And there's the garden centre. That makes an increasing contribution. Though it really ought to expand, to maximise profits. Only I haven't got the capital. So it stays as it is.'

She took a sliver of smoked cheese and nibbled at it. 'What about your father? Can't he help?'

Rupert gave her an incredulous look. 'Dad? He's more likely to ask *me* for money.'

'Oh.' She thought. 'Well, what about the rest of your family?'

Rupert grinned. 'Every word you say shows how little you know about my family. My father is a gambler and a playboy—exactly what your father thought of me, I imagine. He is charming, feckless, extravagant and just a little bit crooked. Not a great provider of capital. My mother is his exact female counterpart, which I suppose is why she left him. They simply couldn't afford each other. They were both only children, so there are no aunts and uncles. One or two cousins are knocking around but they've got hardened to lending Dad's branch of the family money. They know they won't get it back. And my grandmother . . .' He paused.

'Yes?' Cressida prompted, intrigued.

'You might like my grandmother,' he said, a faint, private smile playing about his mouth. 'You might like her a lot.'

'Would she lend you money to expand the garden centre?'

'Good God, no. She doesn't want to know anything about business. And anyway, she wouldn't lend money to a man. A woman, possibly.' He considered it.

Cressida was faintly put out. 'And I would like her? She sounds pretty sexist to me.'

'Totally,' Rupert agreed cordially. 'My grandmother was a musical comedy star and married my grandfather though he was thirty years older than herself. She regards men as net providers of the good things of life.'

Cressida pushed her chair back. 'I don't think we would have very much in common,' she said crisply. 'I don't expect a man to provide me with anything. I am quite capable of earning my own living.'

Rupert did not move, regarding her lazily across the table. 'Not anything?' he echoed softly. 'That seems a shame.'

Cressida sniffed. 'You know what I mean.'

'Yes.' His tone was suddenly bleak. 'For my sins, I do.' He began to play with an unused fork, spinning it in his fingers and releasing it, before spinning it in the opposite direction, apparently bending all his concentration on it. 'I could wish you understood me equally well,' he remarked.

She frowned, trying to make sense of it. Was he

saying that there was, after all, an ulterior motive in his offer of friendship? In spite of appearances, did he want something from Jerome Sebastian and think that Cressida was the best route to it? She passed their conversation that evening under review. The garden centre! It needed capital. Did Rupert think that she might be able to persuade her father to invest in it? Perhaps even make the investment herself? If so, he was probably right, though Cressida's heart sank at the thought. She was not quite sure why. After all, she was used to such approaches.

To disguise it, she said in her most businesslike voice, 'I'm not a mind-reader. If you have proposals to make, let me have the details and I'll see what can be done.'

Rupert gave a crack of laughter, getting lazily to his feet. His chair tipped up and fell in a tipsy position against the wall. He ignored it.

'Right,' he said in a voice of unholy amusement. 'If that's the way you want it.'

He strolled round to her and stood by her chair, his eyes glinting down at her, one hand on its back. Cressida met his eyes. Besides amusement, there was a distinctly determined air to him. She realised suddenly how very firm that beautiful mouth could become.

She swallowed, suddenly and inexplicably nervous. He was drawing her chair further away from the table, holding out a hand to help her rise. Bemused, she took it and stood, unable to wrench her eyes from his.

'So,' said Rupert gently, spinning the chair away from them and putting his hands on her shoulders. 'My proposal is bed. Now.' His voice deepened mockingly. 'What do you think can be done about that?'

CHAPTER NINE

THE office was very quiet. All the people who had come to the meeting Cressida had called to discuss Michael Forest's paper had left. There was a full ashtray on a side table, several empty glasses and a disarray of the normally precisely placed chairs. The room looked devastated, worn out, and the silence was the aftermath of the storm.

Cressida looked eloquently at her secretary.

'That was difficult,' said Lesley, shutting her notebook with a snap. She hesitated and then said, 'I understand that Mr Jerome has been telephoning senior executives personally.'

'That,' said Cressida wearily, 'is obvious.'

She leaned back in her chair, closing her eyes and pressing her fingertips to her temples. The headache that had been hovering for three days had become a pounding pain. She picked up her glass of water and found it dry, replacing it with a grimace. Looking up, she found Lesley watching her with concern.

'You're not well, are you?'

Cressida shrugged it off. 'I'm tired and frustrated and angry with my father. I'm also——' she chose her words with care '—pretty shaken at discovering that I don't really run Sebastian U.K. Oh, it's fine as long as I run my father's errands. He's quite happy to call me Managing Director then. But if I oppose him—even for very good reasons—he doesn't listen; he just snatches the reins back into his own hands.'

Lesley, who was nothing like as surprised as Cressida had been at Jerome Sebastian's reaction to opposition, murmured sympathetically.

Cressida sighed and sat up, rotating her shoulders, then stretched her arms above her head.

'Oh well, I'd better start looking for another job, I suppose.'

Lesley was so startled she dropped her notebook.

'You'd *leave*?'

'I doubt if I'll have much choice,' Cressida said with irony. 'The only contest is whether I can get away before my father kicks me out.'

Knowing her affection for her father, Lesley looked shocked. 'Surely he wouldn't do that?'

'If I don't capitulate, yes, he will.'

'Then—surely—it would be better to do what he wants. It's his company, after all.'

Cressida's mouth took on the obstinate line it had shown all through the stormy meeting.

'He wants to run down that little company, throw fifty people out of work, and all so that he can strip out the property assets, thereby making himself fractionally richer than he is already. It's immoral. I won't have anything to do with it.'

'But—to resign ... Mr Sebastian would be so hurt,' objected Lesley.

'That,' said Cressida, 'is his own fault.'

Lesley bit her lip. She was fairly sure she knew what was behind this determination of Cressida's to defy her father and it filled her with apprehension.

'All for Lord Dearham?' she blurted out. 'Is he really worth it?'

Cressida sat bolt upright as if she had received an electric shock. Her face stiffened.

'I beg your pardon?' she said softly.

Lesley looked miserable. 'I'm sorry. I didn't mean to upset you. But he's your *father*,' she said, not very coherently.

'Lord Dearham?' queried Cressida, eyes bright and hard as agates. 'How curious. I wouldn't have thought he was old enough.'

'I didn't mean that. You know what I meant,' muttered Lesley.

'On the contrary, I am completely in the dark. Perhaps you would like to explain,' Cressida said icily.

'All right then, I will.' Lesley was very fond of Cressida but she had her fair share of spirit and did not like being spoken to in that haughty voice. 'Ever since you met Rupert Dearham you've been behaving like a teenager. Well, that's fine, it's time you did. It's nobody's business but your own. But you're just being stupid, if you're intending to throw up your career and break with your father because of a man like that.'

The freezing face told her nothing. If there had been one tiny sign of emotion, Lesley would have stopped there, but Cressida was giving away nothing. From the expression on her face one would have thought she was faintly bored by the conversation.

'For one thing, *he* won't want you if you break with your father,' said Lesley, goaded. 'He's desperate for money, you know. I've been hearing things: he's been after an heiress—any heiress—for a year or more. He won't be interested if you get yourself disinherited.'

'I assume you are still speaking of Lord Dearham?' asked Cressida in a remote voice.

'Oh Cress, don't pretend. Not with me. You've been a changed person since you met him. And he simply isn't worth it,' said Lesley sadly.

'You know him well?'

'I don't have to know him well,' Lesley cried. 'I can see it. Who do you think leaked that story to the papers about you spending the night with him? On two occasions,' she reminded Cressida. 'That's what it said. Once in London, at your flat, once in Oxfordshire at his place. That wasn't some bribed servant, was it? Not at two separate places. It had to be one of the people involved. And from your face when you saw the column, I'd guess it wasn't you.'

'You think Lord Dearham fed that story to the gossip writer? But why?'

Lesley looked miserable, her eyes falling away from Cressida's clear gaze. She shuffled her papers.

'Why?' persisted Cressida ruthlessly.

Lesley dipped her head. 'To force your hand,' she muttered. She looked up suddenly, almost defiantly, and went on, 'I know how you feel about marriage. I suppose he didn't. And when you turned him down, he thought that if he plastered you all over the papers, your father would try to persuade you to marry him.'

Cressida felt as if she had been dipped in acid. Every nerve shivered at Lesley's words. But all she said was, 'Your pronouns are a little complicated but I get your drift. And you are quite wrong.' She gave Lesley a level look. 'Rupert Dearham has never asked me to marry him. Nor do I expect that he ever will.'

Cressida walked to the window as Lesley left the room without speaking. Down in the courtyard she could see people hurrying off to lunch. She envied them their purposeful steps, their obvious destinations. They contrasted sharply with her own feeling of helplessness. It was as if she were a piece of flotsam caught in a stream, being turned and eddied in directions she had not chosen and could not resist. Between Keith, who was dogging her footsteps, and her father, who telephoned her almost hourly, she felt buffeted. And the worst thing was that Rupert Dearham had not seen her nor spoken to her nor, as far as she could discover, made any attempt to do so since that night.

She leaned forward tiredly and rested her brow against the cool glass. No, as she had told Lesley, Rupert would never ask her to marry him. He probably never wanted to see her again; not after that night.

She shuddered, remembering. Why had she allowed herself to go so far? Why had she given in to the undeniable temptation of Rupert Dearham's charm and

wit? She was not a child, not an innocent. It was not the
first time that her seduction had been attempted. She
had always extracted herself from the situation before.

She grimaced. Well, she had extracted herself from it
this time, but too late to salvage any dignity or self-
respect or to leave Rupert with any feelings for her but
the sort of pitying disgust she had seen on his face
when, at last, she was begging him to let her go. Oh,
why had she let it go so far? Why had she not left as
soon as he made his laughing suggestion?

It would have been so easy. He must have been
expecting it, even. Why, oh why, had she stayed there
staring up at him, silent and breathless as a starstruck
teenager?

'No reply?' Rupert had teased her silence. He had run
one finger lightly down her cheek and watched with
pleasure the little tremor of reaction. 'You can hardly
claim no response, can you? So what are you going to
do about it, efficient Mrs Harley? I await your detailed
programme.'

He had been laughing at her. Cressida knew he was
laughing at her. Desperately she had reached for her
own sense of humour, for something to bring her back
into equilibrium. In vain.

'No? Then it seems to be my decision,' Rupert had
said, not noticeably put out. 'And I think it's time I
showed you my private apartments.'

That was when she should have gone. Then, when he
put an arm round her and guided her, gently but with
great firmness, out of the kitchen and up the well-lit
staircase to a panelled door. Instead she had stood
beside him in acquiescing silence, as he took out a
bunch of keys from his pocket, unlocked the door and
closed it softly behind them. She had only the briefest
glimpse of the room, which appeared to be some sort of
sitting-room, full of books and comfortable chairs, with
a desk in the window and a sofa next to the fireplace.

And then Rupert was holding her, kissing her, and she saw nothing but the wild, whirling colours behind her closed eyelids.

She had responded to him. He was quite right about that. The depth of her response startled Cressida herself. For those heady minutes she forgot everything but the quickened pulse in her body, driven by his, driving his. Her limbs flexed and arched under his touch, recognising their fellow. She gave him kiss for kiss, sharing his demand, sharing the near ferocity, sharing the overwhelming sense of need.

When he finally let her go she was breathless and dazzled.

'Excellent!' Rupert's eyes were dancing. He had sounded warm, amused, appreciative but not—Cressida noted with something like pain—not moved. He was pleased with her response, even faintly surprised by it, but he was not rocked off balance. 'Progress indeed,' he had congratulated her, kissing the tip of her nose and drawing her to the sofa, where he had drawn her comfortably into his arms as they sank among its cushions.

Well, of course he had not been off balance. He was an international sophisticate who had been through this sort of encounter thousands of times. She knew that. She would have guessed it, even if she had not had his reputation in the gossip columns to go by. It was ridiculous to expect him to be as startled by passion as she was herself. Startled and faintly frightened.

'Progress?' she had murmured enquiringly. It was said against his skin.

His arms had tightened.

'For a lady who, by her own account, "doesn't like sex",' Rupert had reminded her, still gently laughing.

She had stiffened. She had forgotten she had told him that. Perhaps he had regarded it as a challenge, an irresistible opportunity to try his hand at the seduction of a lady who was not, at least to begin with, as willing as his usual partners. For she was willing enough now, in all conscience.

Chilled, Cressida had struggled a little to free herself. Rupert had let her go easily enough. She had more trouble with the cushions than with the force of his arms. She had sat up, smoothing her hair with shaking fingers, while he had lain back watching her, smiling.

She had said with difficulty, 'I—don't usually behave like this.'

'Then I am flattered.' The words had been straightforward enough but she could see that his lips twitched.

She had flushed, looking away.

Rupert had not been at all discomposed, she could see that. He did not think that the fact that she had broken the kiss and retreated from his arms mattered in the slightest. She would still end up in his bed, making love with him. Her present retreat was no more than a temporary setback, hardly even that. There was confidence in every line of him, from the long arm thrown casually along the back of the sofa, to the lazy, glinting eyes that surveyed her so watchfully. For a moment Cressida had almost hated him for that confidence.

'Rupert, I don't want . . '

'Hmm?' He had seemed hardly to be listening. He had put out a hand and tucked the hair back, very gently, behind her ear. Cressida had stopped dead, as if she'd been burned. 'You were saying?'

She had swallowed, her mouth suddenly dry. She had not answered. She had not thought she was capable of speech and she was almost certain that Rupert knew it; had deliberately brought it about. That was the depth of his expertise, she had thought bitterly. That was how completely he was in control, as if she were an instrument that he knew how to play. Cressida had resented it fiercely.

He had shifted slightly, drawing her gently but quite inexorably towards him. His hand had slid under the loose blouse, massaging her shoulder gently before it went on to slide the garment away from her. At some point he must have undone the buttons. Cressida had been startled as the silk fell, flowing away from her body like water and as irretrievable. She had grabbed for it too late. He had caught both her hands between his and given them a little tug. She had toppled forward to lie against his chest.

Rupert had given a soft laugh at her helplessness. He had kissed her ear fleetingly. His hands had travelled the length of her exposed spine before dealing unhurriedly with the fastenings of her skirt. Cressida had begun to shiver as she felt his fingers on the long revealed length of her thighs.

He was masterly at this, she had thought. He had done it too well, too often. And she was too inexperienced. She had no hope of getting away from him then. The most frightening thing was that she did not even want to. Though she had been as tremulous as a schoolgirl under those clever hands she was, she suddenly realised, no longer afraid. She had wanted everything that he was offering, was urgent to give, in her turn, all that he required of her.

Rupert had moved, making her lift her head from his chest, gazing deep into her eyes. Of her own free will Cressida had leaned forward and touched her mouth to his, shyly, gravely. He had given a long sigh.

And then they were kissing fiercely, in a frenzy. She had pressed her body hungrily against him, shaking. His hands on her body had no longer been skilful but hard and even a little clumsy in their haste. Cressida had been hardly aware that the pressure was hurtful. She had turned and moaned in a sudden imperative need, her own hands desperate, running up and down the clenching muscles of his shoulders as if to imprint herself on him for ever.

'Darling,' he was muttering. 'Darling Cressida. Yes. Oh yes. Touch me. Want me. Forget him. I'll make you forget him. I can give you so much more.'

His kisses had been deep. She had barely heard the words between them. She was all sensation, starving for him. There was a tremor, a savage fluttering, in the very centre of her body which was somehow an echo of his heartbeat and yet not an echo for it matched exactly. They were like two alien craft, broadcasting different call signs on different wavelengths and then modifying them, slowly, to match, to synchronise . . . The force of that mutual rhythm was appalling. Cressida had felt it pounding through her whole length. Her head was full of it.

Very slowly, his hand possessively on her hip, Rupert had moved. He had stripped away her last remaining scrap of clothing with deliberation. He had looked down at her. Cressida had lain very still, lips parted, her breath coming painfully. She was, she realised, way out of her depth. A flutter of apprehension had taken her again.

Rupert must have seen something of that fleeting fear. His eyes had narrowed.

'Forget him,' he had said harshly.

She was confused. Forget him? Who? Her father? Why should she be thinking of her father at a time like this? She had moved her head against the cushions in a slow negative movement, denying the implication.

He had drawn an audible breath. 'You don't give quarter, do you?' Rupert had said in an oddly ragged tone.

Cressida had not understood him. But his words had recalled all too vividly another man in another country. Keith too had complained that she did not give, that she was selfish and unloving. That she was cold.

Pain, as sharp as a physical convulsion, had assaulted her and made her flinch. Instantly Rupert had stilled. Cressida had looked away from him miserably, no longer able to meet his eyes.

All those echoes of the past that she had so long refused to listen to started to murmur in her ear: dull, frigid, hard. 'You're the most sexless woman I've ever met, Cressida: why can't you even *try*?' All those nights when she had waited in the flat, tense and alone, for Keith to come back; she had pushed them down, out of her conscious memory, but they were flooding back now. Keith would come in late and, sometimes, rather drunk and they would talk in brief, barbed phrases like hostile diplomats. And then, later, when she had gone to bed, leaving him with his briefcase full of work and his bottle full of whisky, she would hear him lurching along the corridor to their room and her heart would turn to marble in her breast.

Oh God, he had been right when he said she was cold: she had felt cold and hard as quarried rock. Sometimes, in his frustration, he had been hurtful but she, though she hated it and him, had not felt injured. She had felt rather as if he were bruising himself on her, dashing himself to pieces against her disgust. She had learned to fear and hate herself in those violent nights before Keith finally stopped trying to make love to her.

And now there she had been with Rupert Dearham, who had offered her his friendship, ready to do it all again. She would hurt him. She was sure of it. She had been able to sense it already. The lazy, loving smile was gone, the clear eyes steeply hooded. And though his hand had rested on her hip it had lain there with a heavy deliberation as if all sponaneity had evaporated.

In a gesture that was pure reflex, Cressida had covered her face with her hands.

Very gently, Rupert had removed them.

'Don't hide from me,' he had said.

She had not been able to look at him. She had been miserably conscious of all the things that, only moments ago, had seemed natural: her nakedness, her disturbed breathing which nothing could disguise, the weight and warmth of his body. She had bitten her lip in distress, overwhelmed by shyness. There was a long silence.

When he had spoken, Rupert's voice had been very soft and controlled, as if he were making a deliberate attempt to control some strong emotion. Cressida had sensed anger—she had faced anger so often from Keith, anger and that sneering contempt—and had shrunk.

'Cressida Harley, let's get one thing clear. I want to make love to you.' The firm mouth had moved in a wry smile. 'There can't be much doubt about that. Provided you want me too, I *will* make love to you.'

He had paused but Cressida still had said nothing. She was prey to too many emotions to know what she wanted or even what she was feeling, beyond a horrifying shame. She was ashamed of everything she was and everything she had done. It was she who had led Rupert to this place, she knew it. He was much too cool and aware to have stampeded her. She had come here consenting.

And she had no right to consent, because she was a destroyer. Shivering, she had looked the truth in the face. It was she, just as much as Keith, who had destroyed her marriage; she with her ignorance, her naive expectations, her inflexibility.

Her naked skin had felt cold.

She had said in a low, ashamed voice, 'I can't.'

For a moment he did not speak. Then he had touched her face very gently.

'*Don't* you want me, then?'

It was not in her character to deny it, even if she had any hope of being believed. And after the last few minutes, Cressida had thought wryly, not even the most credulous man in the world would have believed she was indifferent to Rupert Dearham. Rupert, though, was neither credulous nor unaware of the effect he could have on a lady if he put his mind to it.

At the thought of those other ladies, a wave of pure despair had washed through her. It would be worse than Keith, a thousand times worse. She would know from the start that he would not be faithful. She would be braced all the time for it, anticipating it, fearing every passing mood as a signal that it was over. And she would be afraid of them too, her unseen, unknown rivals, and the comparisons he must inevitably draw.

Cressida had shaken her head, more at the images she had conjured up than at Rupert.

'I *can't*,' she had said, with unmistakable sincerity.

He had drawn a sharp breath. Miserably Cressida had turned her head away, knowing she deserved his anger. She remembered all too vividly the things Keith had said to her so often. Rupert would not be as cruel as Keith but he had equal cause and his indifference would hurt no less.

Startling her, Rupert had begun to stroke her jaw, running his thumb along her eyebrow, smoothing it almost absently.

'Can't you?' It was gently said, almost wistful. Cressida's misery had deepened.

'Rupert, I'm sorry ... I wish ...' She had been incoherent, bewildered, torn between the frightening needs of her body, the hard-learned lessons of experience, and a sudden piercing desire to hold him close and give him whatever he wanted. Oh, if only she were not such a coward! If only she did not have such reasons to be. She had said in a tortured voice, 'If only I didn't *remember*.'

The stroking hand had stilled and fallen away.

'Yes,' said Rupert. 'Yes, of course.' He had sounded quite kind but remote and very weary.

He had shifted his weight and she had been free, shivering among the cushions, more with reaction than cold. Cressida had watched him pick up her clothes.

Her heart had ached. More than anything she wanted to put her arms round him and draw him back to her, warming that cool mask of a face back into love, even if it was only a very temporary kind of love. But it was too late then. She had known that without having to be told, Rupert would not let her close again.

She had felt chillingly alone. She had sat up and sunk her head on her arms, clasped about her knees, hiding tears she could suddenly not control.

Her discarded clothes were placed very gently beside her on the sofa. Rupert had not touched her.

'You're shaking,' he had said, still in that remote voice. 'I'm sorry. I never meant to distress you. I thought——' but he had broken off whatever he was going to say. 'Look, I think you'd better stay the night. There are plenty of beds and I'd rather not leave you on your own in this state.' His voice had grown rueful. 'I don't think I've ever had this effect on a woman before. It's very worrying.'

After that he had been faultlessly considerate, thought Cressida, remembering. He had left the room tactfully while she huddled back into her clothes, returning with a mug of some warm drink which she took, obediently, barely tasting it. He had seemed quite at ease, too. There had been no recriminations, no reproaches—or none except in her own head. Eventually, after half an hour or so of casual conversation in which Cressida had tried valiantly to bear her part, Rupert had escorted her to the door of her room where, scrupulously not touching her, he had wished her good night.

And Cressida had spent the rest of the night alone but not asleep, safe but prey to some of the most bitter regrets of her life.

The next morning, oddly, had not been nearly so bad. Rupert had been cheerful. She had suspected, with a little pang at the thought that she would never now find out, that he was a morning person. He had greeted her with unshadowed friendliness, plied her with coffee and taken her to task for failing to eat anything, and then had driven her back through the dew-encrusted fields to the cottage.

She had had plenty of time to get ready for work. She had showered and dressed and packed her briefcase automatically. It had been a wonderful morning, she had noted from her window. The early sun had bathed the landscape in palest gold, striking dewdrops into diamonds. The faint morning chill had not disguised the fact that it would be a scorching day. Cressida had dressed for the weather, thinking that she would never feel warm again.

Before she had left for the station she had checked her answering machine. Somebody had rung, several times apparently, but never left a message. She had shrugged. If it was important, they would no doubt ring again. She had felt no anxiety, she realised with a little shock, because it had seemed to her at the moment that nothing could ever be important again. She had felt anaesthetised to all feeling.

She had got through the day mechanically. Rupert had neither telephoned nor tried to see her. She had slept badly and risen early, eventually going to work on the earliest train.

That was how she had come to miss the newspapers. None had arrived at the station when she had left and she had not thought to buy any when she had reached London. So it had taken Lesley to break the news to her that her night in Rupert's house—her second night with him, as the well-informed gossip-columnist had pointed out—had made it into the press and was causing a mild sensation.

For a while it had seemed to Cressida that she was in the middle of a tornado. The telephone in Lesley's office never stopped and, even though Lesley was too good a secretary to let the enquirers reach Cressida, it was impossible for Cressida to ignore the commotion. And her father, informed by Keith of his daughter's sudden notoriety, began to bombard her with telephoned reproaches and instructions.

Keith, however, had stopped trying to telephone her. He followed her instead. He was at her office when she got back from lunch. She listened to him, told him she had not changed her mind and asked him to leave. He did so. But he was back that evening. Cressida left by the side entrance, feeling like a criminal. It was only a reprieve. He was on the cottage doorstep by nine.

Thinking it was Rupert, Cressida, who was in the garden, had flown to meet him. It was only as she came round the side of the house that she saw Keith. At once, making no sound in her low sandals, she had retreated. Keith had his back to her and was unsuspicious. He rang the bell again but by that time Cressida was departing upstream at a little run. She did not return until she heard the car engine retreating into the summer night.

It set the pattern for the next three days. Reporters lurked in the bushes, Keith stayed at the nearest first-class hotel and her father was never off the telephone. Lesley, initially amused, grew graver during the hours as Cressida tried to maintain her equilibrium and behave as if all this attention was a minor, temporary annoyance.

On the whole, Cressida congratulated herself, she brought it off fairly well. She stayed calm and unflurried at work, firm and regretful with her father, firm and rather more acerbic with Keith. Nobody would guess that when she was alone she was overtaken by fits of violent weeping. Or that she was desperately lonely for the only man in London who did not seem to want to see her or speak to her. For Rupert was silent.

CHAPTER TEN

LESLEY'S coolness did not last long. By the time Jerome Sebastian had rung twice and she had had to call the security force to eject an enterprising photographer from a French magazine who had penetrated the executive floor, Lesley was as full of sympathy as she had ever been.

'It's quite mad,' she said to Cressida, after the photographer, shrugging philosophically, had been led away. 'Why on earth should it *matter* to anyone whether you and Lord Dearham are having a fling or not?'

Cressida pushed a distracted hand through her hair. 'If I knew that, maybe I could stop it.'

'It's extraordinary.' Lesley hesitated, looked at her employer and then said carefully, 'It's almost as if it's being whipped up by someone, wouldn't you say?'

Cressida gave her a wry look. 'I know. I know. It's being orchestrated by the wicked Lord Dearham just so that he can get me to marry him!' she mocked. 'Really, Lesley, your imagination is positively gothic.'

Lesley sniffed but she said no more. It was just as well, for at that moment the door to Cressida's office opened and, very much at home, Keith Harley walked in.

'Good day, Miss Button,' he said, nodding at Lesley dismissively. 'I'm glad I've managed to catch you at last, Cress. We need to talk.'

Cressida sat limply in her executive chair, wondering briefly how many more disasters one day could produce. But she did not let it show.

'Hello, Keith,' she said civilly enough though without enthusiasm. 'I can't give you very long, I'm afraid. I have a meeting. Lesley, will you buzz me when it's called?' she added with a speaking glance.

'Yes, of course,' said the perfect secretary, knowing there was no meeting and resolving to give Keith Harley ten minutes at most. She went out closing the door softly.

Cressida leaned back in her chair. 'Now,' she said, trying not to sound weary, 'what can I do for you, Keith?'

He did not sit. He had always, she recalled suddenly, liked to stand when he was talking to people. Presumably it made him feel more dominant. She had a sudden poignant memory of Rupert sitting at her feet on the grass at his home and swallowed hard. It was not fair to contrast Keith with Rupert.

'You know perfectly well,' he said with something of a snap. 'I must say I've never known you be so difficult, Cress.'

She smiled wryly, mocking her remembered self. 'No, I was always pretty much of a rabbit, wasn't I? I did what you wanted, even when it came to the divorce.'

'You should never have divorced me,' Keith told her irritably. 'It was a great piece of nonsense.'

For a moment Cressida was dumbfounded. '*I* should never have divorced *you*?' she echoed. 'What on earth are you talking about? It was an agreed divorce and you were the one who asked for it.'

Keith dismissed this as an irrelevance. 'I was going through a difficult patch at work,' he said excusingly. He glared at her. 'As you knew.'

Suddenly, the humour of the situation began to dawn on Cressida. She compressed her lips to hide the twitch that she could sense coming.

'I thought you were going through an affair with a blonde computer programmer,' she said innocently.

'She worked in my department!'

'And that made her qualify as trouble at work?' Cressida could not suppress a chuckle. 'You are truly amazing, Keith.'

He flushed. 'If you'd been any sort of wife . . .'

She stopped him. 'But I was,' she said quite softly. '|
was a fully contracted and delivered wife. I came with
the wedding ring, the ten per cent of the company'
shares and the executive vice-presidency.'

'That's very cynical,' he complained.

'It is also the truth.'

He bit his lip. 'You've changed.'

'Have I?' Cressida swung her chair nonchalantly
'Does it surprise you?'

'It's that gigolo of yours,' said Keith on a note of
discovery. 'He has been poisoning your mind against me.

Suddenly all the humour went out of the situation for
Cressida. She went pale with anger. She also went very
quiet.

'Nobody could do that, Keith,' she told him dulcetly

He did not understand. 'I'm glad to hear it. So
perhaps we can at last talk things over sensibly,' he said
with a return to his normal air of complacency.

'Things?' echoed Cressida with dangerous mildness.

'Us,' said Keith unheeding. 'What we do next.'

'Ah. Those things.' Cressida swung a little more
vigorously. 'Well,' she went on in a meditative tone, 'in
the not very distant future, I intend to throw you out.'
She gave him a dazzling smile. 'Permanently.'

Keith stared at her as if she were speaking a foreign
language.

'You don't understand . . .' he began but she
interrupted him ruthlessly.

'On the contrary, I understand perfectly. You
married me on instructions from my father. I was too
stupid to perceive that at the time, so maybe it was not
entirely your fault. Having married me, you felt that
you had done all that was necessary in the way of being
nice to me.'

He looked impatient. 'Cress, I was in a demanding

job. I couldn't jump every time you pulled the strings.'

Five years ago Cressida would have apologised, thought herself in the wrong, kept quiet. Now she looked ironic.

'I wasn't pulling any strings, Keith, and you know it. I could just have done with talking to you from time to time. Maybe even a little affection.'

'You're talking like something out of a woman's magazine,' he said contemptuously. 'Life isn't like that.'

'Isn't it?' She thought of Rupert, involuntarily, of how warm she felt with him, how at home. The glance she bent on Keith Harley was suddenly tinged with pity. 'Well, maybe it isn't for you.'

'It isn't for anyone, no matter what your professional playboy may tell you.'

She leaned back in her chair, her eyes narrowing, her lips smiling.

'Now there,' she said, 'you are wrong. As I now know.' She leaned forward suddenly. 'Now listen to me, Keith. When I married you, I gave you a promise and I meant to keep it. I did my best to keep it. But you were dishonest from the start and I don't think you ever even tried to make a success of the marriage.' She shrugged. 'Well, that was your choice. But don't come whining to me now about how you want to get things sorted out. Being married to you was the most painful time of my life. I'm not going back to it under any circumstances. Even,' she added with sudden viciousness, 'if my father has offered you his entire empire to get me to do it.'

Keith went very red. Cressida noted it with interest. So she had not been mistaken in her suspicions of Keith's sudden change of heart. She wondered absently what it was that her father could have offered him.

He said with abrupt brutality, 'Your father wants a grandson. You're not going to give him one on your own and he certainly won't say thank you for a bastard of Dearham's. You need me, Cress.'

For a moment she was absolutely still. Then she leaned forward and stabbed at her intercom. Before Lesley could speak she said in a shaking voice, 'Mr Harley is leaving. Now.'

He began to bluster, realising too late that he had overplayed his hand. She did not acknowledge him or even so much as look at him, staring straight ahead of her as if he were not in the room.

Lesley appeared at the door, a little shaken. She had never heard Cressida use that tone of voice before.

Keith had one last parting shot at the frozen figure behind the desk.

'He won't want you when Jerome disinherits you. And he will. You wait and see. Dearham's not going to be interested then.'

Cressida did not concede by so much as the flicker of an eyelash that she had heard this spiteful remark. Balked, Keith left, ignoring Lesley's politely murmured farewells and banging the door behind him in a sudden childish display of temper.

'Phew!' said Lesley, looking after him, her surprise for once overwhelming her discretion. She caught sight of Cressida's rigid face and was concerned. 'Was he—unkind?' she asked.

Cressida turned icy eyes on her. 'He was diabolically impertinent,' she said with deliberation. 'If he turns up again, get the security people to throw him out and tell them it's on my authority. I will not see him.'

Lesley swallowed. She tried to picture herself having a vice-president of the Sebastian Corporation forcibly ejected from the building and failed. On the other hand, she recognised that she had never seen Cressida so angry. It was to be hoped, thought poor Lesley, that Keith did not try to see his former wife again, at least not during working hours.

'Er—yes,' she murmured unconvincingly and retreated.

The rest of the day and for the remainder of the week Cressida worked like a demon. The letters and reports poured out of her office. She seemed to be there at all hours and Lesley stopped even expecting to go lunch.

'What's she doing?' asked the young assistant who did the photo-copying, eyeing with disfavour another delivery from Mrs Harley's office. 'Building a nest with photo-copies?'

Her older companion looked thoughtful. 'If you ask me, I'd say she was getting ready to leave. Clearing out the pending tray. I've seen it before. I always know who's going to resign before the management does,' she ended with a touch of satisfaction.

'Resign?' The young photo-copyist did not believe it. 'But she's one of the family.'

The other shrugged, turning back to her machine. 'Maybe she wants to join another family. Seems to be what the papers think.'

'Mmm, yes. I'd leave a lot more than Sebastians for Lord Dearham. He looks a dish.'

'Handsome is as handsome does,' was the answer. 'And if you don't get those papers copied pretty smartly you could find yourself leaving Sebastians for nothing but your month's pay in lieu of notice. So hop to it.'

The girls in the copying bureau were not the only ones speculating on Cressida's future. Most of her fellow directors found time to wander round to her office during the next few days on one pretext or another to ask obliquely about her long-term plans. She was uncommunicative. Nor did Lesley Button prove a fruitful source of information. And there was no announcement from New York.

Jerome in fact had gone surprisingly quiet. Cressida, no longer harangued for twenty minutes at a time by transatlantic telephone, was slightly uneasy. It was unlike her father to take defeat in silence. Indeed, it was unlike him to take defeat at all.

So she was not entirely surprised when, calling in briefly at the London flat one evening, she found herself greeted by an agitated Lucien with the news that her father had arrived and was in the shower.

She nodded, not betraying any misgivings, and handed her coat to the old servant. 'Does he know that I was intending to call here this evening?'

'He asked,' said Lucien looking miserable. 'What could I do?'

Cressida smiled at him reassuringly. 'Tell him the truth, of course. Don't look so worried, Lucien. He may make a spirited attempt to eat me but I'm tougher meat than you think.'

'I hope so,' Lucien said in so dubious a voice that she laughed aloud.

'You obviously think I need some Dutch courage,' she teased. 'Bring me a rum punch into the drawing-room and I'll wait for Papa.'

She did not have long to wait for either. Jerome must have heard her arrival for he came surging into the room virtually on Lucien's heels. His still thick grey hair was damp and he was buttoning his shirt sleeves absently.

'So there you are.' He surveyed her frowningly. 'I want a word with you, madam.'

She took her drink, thanked Lucien with a smile, and crossed to kiss him dutifully. He suffered the caress but did not return it. As soon as the door had closed behind the servant, he burst into speech.

'What the hell do you think you're about, Cressida? Are you trying to ruin me or ruin yourself?'

She stared at him. He made an impatient noise.

'I gather you've been unforgivable to Keith. In front of witnesses,' he shouted, banging one fist on the other in his fury.

Cressida took a step back. 'So?' she said coolly.

'Don't you realise, you stupid girl, you've set everyone talking?' He sat down, suddenly, as if his rage had exhausted him. He looked very drawn, she realised. All at once, everyone is asking me about who succeeds me.'

She looked at him with compassion. He was not a young man and he worked himself at a punishing pace.

'I'm sure it means nothing,' she said gently.

His answering look was full of scorn.

'You don't know what you're talking about,' he said flatly. 'Not the faintest idea. Or you wouldn't have set everyone gossiping like this about you and that young layabout.'

Cressida stiffened. Jerome did not notice.

'Do you know how many times this week some damn fool has asked me whether I'm going to add a title to the notepaper?' he said bitterly. 'Do you? Or whether there is room for both him *and* Keith in the corporation? What are you trying to do, girl? Bankrupt us?'

'I cannot,' said Cressida with precision, 'see any connection between what is laughably known as my private life and your financial affairs.'

Jerome cast his eyes to Heaven. 'You're my daughter, damn it.'

'But not,' she said, 'your slave.'

They glared at each other.

'Have you no sense of loyalty?' demanded Jerome, trying another tack.

'Yes,' Cressida returned promptly. 'But have you?'

His heavy brows snapped together. 'What do you mean by that?'

She sipped her rum punch, turning a shoulder on him and seating herself with composure on the sofa.

'I mean that you have been throwing Keith at me like a shuttlecock on a string,' she said graphically. 'Each time I duck, and each time he whizzes overhead again.' She looked at him very straight. 'You know that he made me unhappy. You know, because I told you, that after the divorce I did not want to see him again, ever. Why did you do it?'

Jerome looked uncomfortable. 'He's a good boy . . .'

'He may be a good vice-president,' said Cressida judicially. 'Believe me, as a husband he is not good news. At least, not for me.'

Jerome tried, and made a very fair attempt, to look pathetic.

'I'm an old man——'

Cressida made a rude noise into her glass and drank a long swallow.

'I am,' he insisted. 'And you're a good child but you're not hard enough, not suspicious enough.' Suddenly all the play-acting fell from him and he really did look concerned. 'I'm not getting any younger, Cress. You need a man.'

She was touched but she was not prepared to let him get away with it.

'We are all getting older. And I have been responsible for myself for a good long time now, Papa.'

His mouth took on an obstinate line. 'You need a man. Every woman does. It's not natural to live on your own.'

'You do,' she pointed out.

'That's different.'

'Of course,' she murmured.

'It is. At my age, one's needs are different,' he said loftily. 'But you—you're still young enough to have a family, a real family of your own.'

Her smile was enigmatic. 'That's what we're talking about then, is it, Papa? Not my needs, but yours. For a grandson.'

'It doesn't have to be a boy,' said Jerome, falling neatly into the trap she had set for him and realising just too late what he had said.

'Broad-minded of you,' she said drily. 'But it does have to be Keith Harley's?'

'He's the best executive I've ever had,' Jerome said simply.

There was a long silence. Cressida put down her drink. She was no longer thirsty, she found, nor so full of bravado.

At last she said quietly, 'I'm sorry, Papa,' and stood up.

'What do you mean?' He was bristling again.

She made a weary gesture. 'I mean, no deal, Papa. You keep Keith, since you seem to want him. I'll go.'

Jerome lost all colour. 'Go where?'

Cressida shrugged. 'Does it matter? None of your rivals, I promise. I can afford to take my time finding another job. I won't embarrass you.'

'You'd *leave*?' He did not believe it.

She raised her head and met his eyes full on. 'I'd do anything rather than marry a man I don't love. Don't forget, I've done it once.'

Jerome winced. 'Cress, you're all I've got.' For a moment he sounded almost desperate.

'I know.' Cressida was not proof against that appeal. The clear eyes were full of hurt and bewilderment. 'I know,' she said wretchedly.

'You married him of your own free will,' he reminded her.

'I know that too.'

'And it wasn't so bad to begin with, was it?' He was beginning to wheedle.

Desperately Cressida flung away from him, catching up her bag and gloves in shaking fingers.

'Don't say any more, Papa,' she said raggedly. 'Not one word. Just hear this and believe it: I will never marry Keith; I will never have his child. You can either accept it, or cut me out of your life and adopt Keith instead. But you can't found a dynasty on us because I won't have it.'

He began shouting then. He was hurt and bitterly

disappointed and he held her to blame for both. She realised that he would do so and stood stoically under the bombardment of insults, neither defending herself nor answering him.

'And as for that gigolo of yours, I'll put him out of business,' he roared. 'I'll finish him. I'll make him wish he'd never met you.'

A muscle moved in Cressida's white cheek, the only sign of reaction, but it was enough for Jerome.

'In fact, I'll ring him up myself this evening and tell him that you're out—out of the corporation and out of my life. I'll tell him you're just another executive on the dole and what's more that you'll get nothing from me, not now, not ever. I'm cutting you out of my will,' he told her, 'tonight. I'll draw it up here and now and have Lucien and Marthe witness it. If you don't care about me as a daughter should, I won't provide for you like a father.'

He finished triumphantly, his colour high. He put one hand on his hip and flung back his head, taunting her. Cressida's eyes were shadowed. She looked at him very gravely for a moment.

Then she said, 'You must please yourself,' and left the room.

Harshly Jerome's voice followed her, 'If you think Rupert Dearham will want you when you're disinherited, you're even more of a fool than I think you are, my girl.'

She did not pause. Lucien was there, hovering anxiously. He helped her into her coat, murmuring. Jerome appeared in the doorway of the drawing room.

'Or do you think he'll take you with nothing?' he sneered. 'For pure love?'

She drew her gloves on and smoothed them over her wrists. Her hands were, she noted absently, shaking badly. She raised her head and looked at her father blindly.

'You will probably not understand this, Papa,' she said, 'but I'd trust Rupert Dearham with my life. He is not mean. He is not calculating. And he would not care about your money. If he wanted me he would take me, as you say, for pure love. Unfortunately,' she drew a breath which hurt and her mouth twisted wryly, 'he does not want me. At least——' and she was recalling vividly his voice and his teasing laughter, the companionship and the uncontrived passion of their last encounter, and her eyes filled with tears. 'Oh God, I'm going to cry,' she said in horror. 'I can't *bear* it. I'm sorry, Papa.'

And she fled, leaving Jerome utterly silenced.

CHAPTER ELEVEN

CRESSIDA walked slowly to the railway station through the evening streets. She felt very shaken. In all her life she realised, she had never ultimately refused to do what her father wanted. She had stood up to him, coaxed him out of his madder schemes, done her best to modify his harsher prejudices. But she had never, until tonight, said flatly that she would rather disengage from him completely than fall in with his plans.

Jerome too, she thought compassionately, would be shaken by that new implacability. In the past she had always been ready to compromise. Cressida bit her lip. But there was no compromise possible on the matter of marriage. And she could never marry Keith Harley. Not now.

The train she usually caught had long gone. The departures board told her that she had twenty minutes to wait before the next one. She sat down on an old iron seat, still feeling slightly dazed.

What was it that had happened to her? She had thought that after her marriage broke up she had grown up, that suddenly her character had formed and set immutably. She had a career and her friends, and she would never trust herself to a man again. Marriage was out of the question for ever.

But now—she had not told her father that she would never marry; just that she would never marry Keith. It was no longer true that she did not want to marry. It bewildered her. She felt as if she did not know herself any more. Yet it was true. The rigid mould had broken, she could feel it, and now she felt shivering and naked without it. Shivering and yet strangely excited.

162

Her train arrived and she boarded it mechanically, still turning over and over in her mind the extraordinary revelation she had just received. Try as she would, she could not disguise from herself the fact that all this upheaval, all this metamorphosis came back to Rupert Dearham. It was he who had shaken her out of her isolation, making her respond to him as a friend and then—slowly but inexorably—as a lover.

Cressida stared out blindly at the pastureland and cornfields through which the train was wending its way. The shadows were long now. The sky was a pale apricot with the dying sun and here and there a star twinkled already. It was beautiful, cool and peaceful, but Cressida was in turmoil.

Yes, she had responded to Rupert as a lover. How could she have thought otherwise? At the very memory of him her heart lifted in her breast. She became aware of a sweet ache, longing to see him, to go towards him in love and trust and be welcomed.

She moved restlessly on her seat, disturbed at the images she had conjured up. Oh, she responded to him all right, she could not deny it. She wanted him too, just as he had said she did. The trouble was that she did not want him temporarily or occasionally. She wanted him in love and trust for ever. And that was not the way he played the game. He had told her so himself with every word, every gesture.

Cressida thought back to that very first dinner party in the London flat. What was it that he had said? Divorce was practically an inherited affliction in his family, something like that. She shivered.

I could not take that again, she thought. It was bad enough with Keith. Divorce from Rupert would finish me. I shall never love anyone the way I love Rupert. So I dare not ... and yet, if only ...

She spent an evil night, torn between I dare not and if only. There was still silence from Rupert, though there were several messages on her answering machine including one from Jemima Quinn. That danced around in her head too as she fought with the sheets and suffocating pillows. By the time she arrived at Sebastian House next morning she had not only been awake for several hours but looked distinctly the worse for it.

It was a fact duly noted by the reporters waiting for her. She shouldered her way through them, half-blinded by the flashes of powerful cameras, not replying to the avid questions that were flung at her as she walked.

In her office she found Lesley, looking pale and faintly red-eyed.

'Did you know?' Lesley asked her at once.

'Know what?' asked Cressida, though she had a fairly clear idea.

Lesley suppressed a quiver in her voice, though her eyes were full of tears. 'Your father's put out a statement. You are relieved of all executive responsibilities in the Sebastian Corporation.'

'Ah.' Cressida sat down on the corner of Lesley's desk and swung a leg thoughtfully. 'And that was all?'

Her secretary stared. 'All? What more were you expecting? That he would put out a contract on you?'

Cressida smiled. 'Not quite. But I thought he might name—er—his successor as Chief Executive.'

'Name Keith Harley, you mean,' said Lesley shrewdly. 'No, there's nothing like that in the announcement.'

'I wonder why not,' Cressida mused. 'Unless he hasn't entirely given up hope? But no, surely not. I was quite definite, last night.' She shrugged, standing up. 'Oh well, no point in staying indoors on a lovely day like this, if I'm not even getting paid for it.' She gave Lesley a mischievous smile. Suddenly she looked very light-hearted. 'Let's get my severance terms sorted out and my desk drawers clear and I'll be off to sit in the sun in my garden.'

It was clear, thought Lesley, that Cressida was neither hurt nor very much surprised by her father's precipitate announcement. She talked in a calm, even voice to the company's solicitor, dictated a factual memo to the Board setting out the terms she was seeking to compensate her for her abrupt departure, and was in the point of leaving, some time after lunch, when Keith Harley stormed in.

'I suppose you think you've been very clever,' he flung at her, ignoring Lesley. He tossed a lunchtime newspaper down on the desk in front of her, so that she could see the blurred picture of herself on the front page.

Cressida raised her brows. 'Clever?'

'Backing Jerome into a corner like that. Did you know he was going to name me First Deputy President in the USA?'

'No,' she said tranquilly. 'But I'm not surprised. And I don't see what that,' she waved a hand at the paper, 'has to do with it.'

'He can't do it now, can he? Can you imagine the field-day the press would have? Son-in-law Cuts Out Ex-Wife,' he enunciated bitterly. 'That would be great for Sebastians' image, wouldn't it? And you know how important image is, in our business.'

She shrugged, not answering. Infuriated, Keith leaned forward, thumping his fist down hard in the offending newspaper.

'Look at me when I'm talking to you, damn it. Do you know what this has done to our share price already?'

Cressida turned round very deliberately and surveyed him. Keith sucked in his breath.

'Or don't you care?' he said softly. 'You'll go to any lengths to thwart me and you don't care if you ruin your own father in the process.'

'Don't be stupid,' said Cressida contemptuously.

But he was so full of rage he was beyond hearing her. 'Do you think that your Lord Dearham will have you after this? Do you? Do you know how much his company is in debt? How much he is in need of money? Do you think that if you ring him now he will *speak* to you?'

Cressida said wearily, 'Keith, I've told you, this has nothing to do with Rupert Dearham.'

He had picked up the telephone and was flourishing the handset at her.

'Go on. Try him. Try your noble lover *now*!'

'But I don't want to talk to him. I have nothing to say,' she protested. 'This is ridiculous.'

'You *dare* not.'

Cressida lost her temper. 'Lesley, get me Queen Anne Place,' she said between her teeth. 'Rupert Dearham's office. At once.'

She and Keith glared at each other while the machine clicked and whirred. They heard the dialling noises, the mutter of conversation, and then a voice saying clearly, 'Lord Dearham's secretary here. May I help you?'

'I'd like to speak to him, please,' said Cressida curtly.

'May I know who is calling?' asked the voice sweetly.

'Cressida Harley.'

There was a perceptible pause. Then the voice, a shade less assured and considerably more embarrassed, said. 'Oh, I'm sorry, Mrs Harley, Lord Dearham is not here just at present. Could I take a message, or perhaps I could help?'

Cressida stared. For a moment she did not answer. She knew that she had not behaved as well to Rupert as she would have liked but she thought he must have known that was because of her pitiful state of confusion. It had never occurred to her that he would refuse to speak to her.

Keith was grinning. 'You see? He reads the papers too. He's realised you're not the blank cheque he thought you were.'

'Hello, Mrs Harley?' said the distant secretary, sounding less and less happy. 'Hello? Hello?'

Slowly Cressida returned the telephone to its cradle.

'Regretting it?' Keith taunted.

She turned cool eyes on him. She was wounded but she was not going to display her hurt for Keith to gloat over.

'My only regret,' she said with precision, 'is ever having had anything to do with you. Goodbye, Keith. I wish you all the luck in the world. Just don't come near me again.'

His lip curled but he turned on his heel and walked out without speaking. Presumably he, too, thought Cressida wryly, saw her as a cancelled cheque. She sat down rather hard in her chair. She looked up to see Lesley in the doorway, her expression compassionate.

'I'm sorry, Cress.'

With an effort Cressida straightened her shoulders. She felt as if she had been physically punched, stiff and sore in all her muscles. It must be shock.

'Yes,' she said quietly. 'So am I. I thought he was different.' She tried to smile. 'But then I would, wouldn't I?' She shook her head a little as if trying to clear it. 'You must have been right all the time.'

Lesley did not look very happy about this admission. 'Maybe he really is out of the office,' she offered.

Cressida's look was ironic. 'Is that what it sounded like to you?'

Lesley bit her lip. 'No.'

'No,' Cressida agreed.

'But there could be some other explanation.'

'There might, yes. Can you think of one off-hand?' Cressida asked politely. She gave her secretary a small smile that, Lesley thought, was the most tragic thing she had ever seen. 'No, neither can I. I imagine Keith was right and he has read the papers and decided to cut his losses. As,' she ended, raising her head proudly, 'I shall do myself.'

Lesley was tempted to protest further, to suggest the Cressida give the absent Lord Dearham the benefit of the doubt, but one glance at the pallor of the composed face and the tearless glitter of the eyes dissuaded her.

Instead she murmured, 'Jemima Quinn rang. She's in the West End and wants you to have tea with her. She said she'd come here.'

For a moment Cressida hesitated. Then she shrugged. 'Oh, well, what difference does it make? What time did she say?'

'Between three and four.'

Cressida looked at her watch. 'Now, in other words.'

It seemed unavoidable. And she had meant to meet Jemima Quinn one day this month anyway, though she would have preferred it not to be today. She would have preferred not to meet anyone today. She felt raw from Rupert's rejection; and Keith's gloating had not made it any easier.

Jemima arrived early and swept Cressida into a waiting taxi and off to Brown's Hotel for tea. She looked a different person from the anxious woman she had been when they last met, Cressida thought. She was wearing a smart new outfit, had had her hair newly styled and was sparkling with energy.

'You're the most cheerful thing I've seen all day,' Cressida told her, after admiring her dress.

'It makes a change. I used to be noted for my ability to spoil parties,' Jemima returned, slipping off her linen jacket and handing it to the waiter. 'It was very, very boring.' She gave a half-smile. 'I think I must have bored you horribly at that dinner party you gave for Lord Dearham.'

Cressida flinched but was spared having to answer by the waiter's leading them to a corner table. They sat in the deep easy chairs while he tenderly placed a cloth over the small occasional table beside them.

'Yes,' Jemima was musing. 'When you're in love

yourself, there is nothing more tedious than being bombarded with troubles of people who are in love no longer.'

Cressida shifted uncomfortably. 'I—wasn't. In love, that is.' Jemima raised disbelieving brows. 'Honestly. It was just business. My father set it up,' said Cressida, a touch desperately. This was worse than she had expected.

'Yes, that's what it looks like from today's papers,.' agreed Jemima, amused. But she changed the subject willingly enough and began to talk about her own affairs. 'It was that party of yours that made all the difference, really. I was at the end of my tether and when you said how unhappy your divorce had made you I thought—well, she must know, perhaps it's worth one last try. It impressed Sefton too, though of course he would never admit it. And he didn't like what Lord Dearham said either—about divorces running in families. He's very attached to the children. He's always been a good father.' She gave Cressida a quick look. 'You and Keith didn't have any children, did you?'

Cressida shook her head. She had never wanted children. Now she realised blindingly that she had not wanted Keith's children. In other circumstances . . . She picked up her teacup and drank quickly, hoping Jemima did not notice the too ready tears that sprang to her eyes.

'Well, Sefton has never wanted to hurt the children. It's been the one thing we agreed about. And after that party, I thought, we have to get this sorted out once and for all. He keeps saying he wants a divorce: let's see if he means it. So I put it to him—you'd been divorced, Rupert Dearham's parents had been divorced. Neither of you seemed happy about it. I told Sefton that if he wanted a divorce I would give him one but, looking at you two, did he really think it was the cure for all ills? Would we not be better off trying to build on what we had?'

Cressida said, 'And he agreed?'

'He agreed. He was impressed by what you said, as I told you. Up till then he'd only been thinking about getting his freedom. Suddenly he started to think about life *after* divorce and found it might not be very pleasant. So,' she gave Cressida a contented smile, 'we're back together again and trying hard. It was a sobering evening for both of us. We owe you.'

Cressida smiled. 'I'm glad,' she said sincerely. 'At least something good came out of that evening.'

Jemima raised her brows. 'You and Rupert Dearham weren't good?'

Cressida flushed, turning her face away. 'Rupert and I were friends, Jemima, no more than that. And that only very briefly.' She gave a harsh sigh.

'Really?' Jemima sounded disbelieving again.

'Really.'

'But that evening he could not keep his eyes off you. I was very envious,' she added. 'I couldn't help remembering how long it was since Sefton had looked at me like that.'

Cressida was dumbfounded. That evening he had been angry, furious with her father's despicable plan and furious at what he thought was her agreement to carry it out. Surely he could not have been attracted to her *then*.

'I think you must be mistaken,' she said.

Jemima shook her head. 'Oh no, I wasn't. You get eagle-eyed about other people's happiness when your own is on the rocks. I saw what I saw. Though,' she added reflectively, 'I was not sure that you had noticed. Presumably he brought it to your attention eventually?'

Cressida swallowed. 'Er—yes.' She held out her cup for more tea. 'But briefly.'

'That's a pity. You seemed so well suited.' Jemima poured tea.

'Did we?' Cressida did not realise how wistful her tone was.

Jemima eyed her thoughtfully for a moment and then leaned forward. 'Look, Cressida, tell me to mind my own business if you like, but has something gone wrong between you? Is it because of the firm?' Cressida shook her head. 'It's quite pointless falling out over work, you know. Sefton and I used to do it all the time. After all, you can change your job—and one day you'll leave it anyway—it's not permanent in the way relationships are—or are supposed to be,' she ended wryly.

'Some relationships,' Cressida corrected her.

'All right. Some. Like mine and Sefton's. The important ones. Isn't Rupert Dearham important to you?'

'I——'

'Isn't he? Truly?'

Cressida dipped her head. 'Yes, he is,' she allowed in a low voice.

'So there you are. You can't let Sebastians come between you.'

Cressida shook her head. 'It isn't Sebastians,' she said miserably. 'It's me. Or at least it was. Now—' she spread her hands hopelessly, 'now I don't know any more.'

'Explain,' said Jemima, frowning.

'Well, to begin with, I was afraid,' Cressida said hesitantly. 'I suppose that was it. The divorce messed me up rather and I didn't want to get involved again. Everybody knew that. Nobody had tried for years——' she broke off, flushing.

'Until Rupert ignored the warning notices and broke through to you?'

'I—yes.'

'And then what happened?'

'I turned him down,' Cressida said flatly, seeing in her mind's eye the events of that last encounter and bitterly regretting them. 'I led him on and then turned him down.'

'And he was angry? Bitter?'

'No,' she said slowly on a wondering note. 'No. He was very—understanding. More so than I deserved.'

'Guilt,' said Jemima, diagnosing with a professiona air. 'Very destructive. And self-indulgent. You must ge rid of your guilt. Go and talk to him.'

Cressida came back to the present. 'I've tried,' she said simply.

'And?'

'And he would not talk to me. His secretary made a poor job of telling me he was out. Keith——' she swallowed something jagged and painful in her throa '—Keith said that Rupert would not want me once he knew I was out of favour with my father.'

Jemima received this information impassively. 'And you believed him?'

She shrugged unhappily. 'It seems reasonable.'

Jemima sat back in her chair. 'You know, I think you're judging him by your first husband. From what I gather, Keith should have married your father, not you Rupert is not like that.'

'You know him well?' Cressida asked ironically.

'I've watched him watching you,' Jemima reminde her. 'I know where his interests lie.' She sipped her tea watching Cressida over the rim of her teacup. 'I think you ought to go and see him. Beard him in his den Don't give any more secretaries the chance to chok you off. Go and sit on his doorstep.'

Cressida paled at the thought. 'But—he——'

'The worst he could do would be to throw you out, Jemima said bracingly. 'At least then you'd know for sure.' She looked at Cressida with sudden gravity. 'I it's important it's worth taking a few risks for, Cressida I've found that out. All you've got to do is decide how important it is.'

Cressida looked down at her hands. 'It's my whole life,' she said softly, and not just to Jemima.

CHAPTER TWELVE

THE approach to the house, through that fairy-story wood, was more intimidating on your own. Cressida drove through it very slowly, flinching every time a twig brushed against her car or the tyres lurched on a rut. She was very nervous.

It had taken all her courage to walk out of the cottage and into her car this evening. She had had no word from Rupert and she was not even sure whether he would be in the Oxfordshire house this evening. He spent a lot of his time in London; he could still be there. Or he could be abroad again. All the way in the car she had been trying to decide whether it would be worse if Rupert were not there and she had to return frustrated or if he were in residence and she actually had to talk to him. For she had not the slightest idea what she should say. All she knew was an overwhelming need to see him again.

There were no lights in the windows that she could see as she pulled the car gently round the last bend of the drive. So perhaps he was not here. But then, as the engine died and she sat still in the warm evening air, she heard voices. So he was here but he was not alone.

Cressida got out reluctantly. That possibility had never occurred to her. She stood doubtfully by the car. She did not know what to do. Now she heard his deep tones in the distance she realised how desperate she was for a sight of him. On the other hand, she feared his anger, and worse his rejection, quite as much as she wanted to see him.

The decision was taken out of her hands. Rupert himself appeared round the side of the house and stopped dead, staring at her as if he did not believe his eyes

Cressida smiled weakly. 'Good evening.'

He recovered himself. 'A splendid evening,' he agreed, drawling. He strolled across to her, his expression enigmatic. 'And what are you doing with it' Driving around the beauty spots of the county?'

Cressida swallowed. 'I wanted to see you,' she said baldly.

There was an unnerving silence. The hooded eyes told her nothing. Rupert seemed quite relaxed, smiling gently, one hand in the pocket of his cord trousers. By contrast she was as tense as a coiled spring. She could think of nothing more to say though she searched her mind frantically.

At last he said, 'Do you?'

This was worse than anything she had imagined on her way here. She said miserably, 'Yes.'

He shifted slightly. 'Now why, I wonder?'

She felt the heat rise in her cheeks but she met his eyes very straight. 'As you said to me on a previous occasion, I believe I owe you an apology,' she told him

Rupert was very still. 'Ah. But that, as I'm sure you must have realised, was just an excuse to see you again. His tone was light.

'No.' Cressida was dazed. 'No, I didn't realise it.' She looked at him in dawning dudgeon. 'And you *did* owe me an apology.'

He laughed. 'Oh, certainly. But if I hadn't realised that I was rapidly becoming obsessed by you, you wouldn't have got it.'

She was so startled by this cool statement that she gave a wholly unexpected choke of laughter.

'You're outrageous,' she told him.

'So they say. And I think I'm a simple fellow who happens to be honest.' He sighed theatrically. 'Of course, there's not a lot of honesty about.'

Instantly she felt as if he had accused her and stopped

smiling.

'No,' she agreed with constraint.

He looked at her narrowly. '*Now* what have I said?' he began impatiently and then turned his head in a listening attitude.

'You're not alone,' said Cressida awkwardly. 'I've come at the wrong time.' She put a hand on the car door handle. 'I'll go.'

At once he was beside her, his hand closing hard over hers so that it was crushed against the metal painfully.

'You're going nowhere.' In spite of that swift move and the force of his grip on her hand, the smile he gave her was lazy. 'Not until I've got my apology.' He dislodged her hand from the car and clasped it, twining his fingers through hers. 'Come and have a drink and meet my grandmother. When she goes to bed, we can talk. And you,' his eyes fixed blatantly on her mouth and his voice deepened in amusement, 'can apologise appropriately.'

Cressida felt the colour slide warmly into her cheeks. That intimate look made her breathless yet, at the same time, absolutely secure. What a fool you are, she adjured herself, reacting so strongly to a word, a look, no more. But she let her hand rest in Rupert's and went with him obediently.

He took her to the little lawn outside the kitchen where they had sat that last evening. There was a tray with a bottle and two glasses in it and a lady, very upright in a long black skirt and high-necked blouse, sitting in the garden seat. Cressida faltered but Rupert was having no hesitation.

'My grandmother,' he said, marching her towards this presence. 'Polly, this is Cressida.'

His grandmother had a ferociously lined face and the most lively blue eyes Cressida had ever seen. She surveyed the new arrival for an unnerving couple of seconds and then held out both hands.

'How nice to meet you.' Her voice was quellingl
ladylike but she had a twinkle. 'I've heard far too muc
about you. Come and give me your side of the story.'

Cressida jumped and looked at Rupert in alarm. '
don't——' she began but Rupert was laughing.

'Polly, don't be a beast. You're not supposed to tel
all my secrets the moment you meet the girl.'

'But of course I am,' said Polly serenely. 'Why els
did you confide in an old woman? You certainly didn'
want my advice. You never do.' She picked up th
bottle by its neck and waved it at him. 'We nee
another one of these.'

'Certainly.' He gave her a little bow and lounged of
towards the house.

Polly narrowed her remarkable eyes after him. 'On
thing I like about Rupert: he's never slow to take a cue
So unlike his poor father and as for his grandfather—
man with the worst timing I've ever met in my life.' Sh
turned back to Cressida and smiled. 'So you're here a
last. I thought you would come but Rupert wouldn'
have it. He told me he had ruined everything. Com
and tell me about it.'

Feeling as if she needed to get her breath back
Cressida crossed slowly to the intimidating lady an
slipped down to the grass beside her.

'Very pretty,' said Polly approvingly. 'I like gracefu
gels. So many of the gels these days move like electri
mice.'

She had her grandson's gift of surprising her audienc
into laughter, Cressida thought, chuckling and feelin
much more at her ease. She remembered that Ruper
had said his grandmother had been a music-hall sta
and found she could well believe it.

She said demurely, 'Thank you.'

'So tell me what you're doing here tonight. Have yo
decided to forgive him for hurting you, then?'

Cressida stared at her. 'Hurting me?'

'Rupert,' reported his grandmother, 'said he had hurt you so badly you would never speak to him again.'

Cressida's look was blank.

'I see he got it wrong,' said Polly tolerantly. 'They usually do.'

'They?' Cressida was now totally lost.

'Men.' Polly smiled indulgently. 'Particularly the ones who think they understand women. It makes them careless.' She looked down at Cressida with sudden shrewdness. 'Do you think Rupert is careless?'

'I—no. I hadn't thought about it,' Cressida said in bewilderment.

'Well, I can tell you: he isn't. Never has been, not from a child.' She tapped the wooden seat beside her to emphasise her point. 'He's always known exactly what he wanted and how he was going to get it. Long as I've known him.' She held Cressida's eyes. 'And he's always wanted to avoid marriage,' she finished deliberately.

Cressida felt slightly sick. But she managed not to lose her smile and said steadily, 'You do not surprise me.'

Polly gave a sudden, unexpected crack of laughter. 'So. You're a realist. That's a good thing.' She was serious suddenly. 'He tells me you're divorced. Often?'

For a moment Cressida did not understand her. Then, when it dawned on her what Polly was asking, she shook her head violently. 'No. I've only been married once.'

'I've been married five times,' Polly said tranquilly. 'One gets in the habit of it, I find. It suited me. Wouldn't suit Rupert.'

'It wouldn't do for me either,' said Cressida with profound feeling.

There was a little silence while Rupert's grandmother inspected her very hard and Cressida tried to appear unconscious of the fact. Eventually Polly sat back with a little sigh.

'I hope you've come to ask him to marry you,' she said, startling Cressida finally out of her much-tried self-possession.

'What?'

But Rupert was returning from the house with another bottle and a glass. Cressida was faintly appalled. If his grandmother would say such outrageous things to her, what might she unleash on Rupert now that he had arrived? Nothing in the sparkling expression of Polly's bright eyes reassured her. She shifted uneasily as Rupert joined them.

'I hope that's cold enough,' said Polly briskly. 'I can't bear warm Sauvignon.'

'It is,' said Rupert, calmly extracting the cork and pouring wine into his grandmother's glass before filling the fresh one and handing it to Cressida. 'I put six bottles in the fridge when you rang me to say you were inviting yourself down.'

'You didn't expect me to stay long?' asked Polly provocatively.

He grinned at her. 'Only as long as my cellar lasts.'

She nodded, apparently not in the least insulted. 'I like your wine, dear boy. You have inherited your grandfather's palate. It is the only resemblance I have ever detected. Fortunately for you, Cressida. I may call you Cressida? Such a pretty name.'

Cressida blushed, not at the compliment, and found to her indignation that Rupert was laughing at her gently over his glass.

Polly stood up. 'I shall take my wine indoors and rest,' she announced. 'I will see you in the morning, Rupert. And you too, I hope, Cressida.' She nodded at the embarrassed intruder, patted Rupert's cheek lightly and gathered her skirt in one hand professionally. 'I have told her to ask you to marry her,' she remarked casually, as she left. 'She seems a sensible girl. Good night.'

She left in a cloud of very expensive French perfume. Cressida stared down at her wine in an agony of confusion.

'Did she really?' asked Rupert in a strangled voice.

'Really what?' Cressida could not look at him.

'Tell you to propose to me?'

'Er—yes.' She swallowed. 'J-just before you joined us, actually.'

'Dear God,' he said devoutly.

She looked up then. He had dropped his head between his hands, the fair hair falling negligently over his fingers, and his shoulders were shaking. For a moment Cressida was alarmed. Then she realised that he was laughing. Her hand, which had half gone out to him, fell back to her side. She was blushing again, she thought, furious with herself and helpless to prevent it. Where, oh where, was her famed poise?

'Heaven help a man with a family,' he said, when he could speak. 'I'm sorry, she's an interfering old bat.'

Cressida demurred. 'She seems very fond of you.'

'She is. And I adore her,' Rupert agreed cordially. 'She just has no tact.'

'That's not very fair when she has gone inside to rest at,' Cressida consulted her watch, 'ten past nine of a fine evening.' She met his eyes and a fugitive smile warmed her own. 'I call that tact of a high order.'

He looked at her for a long moment, the corner of his mouth curling in amusement. Then he said, 'You could be right. If she wanted to give you the opportunity to propose to me.' He watched with pleasure as Cressida bit her lip, her eyes falling. 'Are you going to?'

She shook her head.

He sighed. 'No, I thought you probably weren't. What *did* you come here for? If it's to accuse me of selling tales to the newspapers, I'm innocent. I can even prove it.'

There was the faintest trace of bitterness in his voice.

Cressida heard it and was confused all over again. Was he resentful of her, after all? Did he mind her coming here this evening uninvited? Yet he had seemed so genuinely welcoming.

She said, 'I don't understand.'

'Don't you?' He drank. 'Didn't the good Miss Button tell you what she told me?' He looked at her over the top of his glass and then shrugged. 'No, I can see that she didn't. Well, I'll tell you. She did some private research into that first story in the papers about you spending the night here. And she discovered the source: a man. A man who knew you very well. Implication: me.'

Cressida said suddenly and clearly, 'I don't believe it. You wouldn't. Not when you know how much I would hate it.'

Rupert's eyes narrowed. 'So you know that much, at least?'

She said urgently, 'She never told me, honestly. Oh, she made no secret of the fact that she believed it was all your doing but I told her I didn't believe it and that was an end of it. She never even suggested that she'd got any proof. And if she had . . .'

'Yes?'

'If she had, I still wouldn't have believed it,' Cressida said softly. 'I may not be the most sensible woman in the world about men but I know you better than that.'

He reached out and took her hand, squeezing it silently. 'You make me ashamed.'

She shook her head, bewildered. 'Why?'

'Your trust. I should have trusted *you*. Instead of stamping off in a fit of pride and refusing to come near you until I could prove that it wasn't me.'

Slow understanding began to dawn. 'Was that why you wouldn't speak to me today?'

Rupert looked uncomfortable. No, he looked more than uncomfortable, he looked as if he were in pain. Cressida said in harsh anxiety, *'Why?'*

He put his glass down on the grass very carefully. 'I could have proved to you several days ago that it was not me.'

She watched his bent head as he turned the glass round and round absorbedly. She began to tremble. She could not guess what was wrong but she was sure that she was now very near the heart of something important.

She said, 'Then why didn't you? If you didn't know that I already believed you innocent, anyway. Or didn't you care what I thought?'

The heavy lids lifted. His eyes blazed. 'You know that's not true.'

'Then why?' He said nothing when she paused. She prodded harder. 'If you had proof.'

He stood up, sharply, angrily, pushing himself away from the ground in a lithe, muscular movement. Cressida stared up at him. He turned his back on her. Realisation began to come.

She said slowly, 'It wasn't just a journalist's lucky streak, was it? It *was* a tip-off.' His shoulders tensed and he thrust his hands into his pockets, not answering. 'Was it Keith?' she asked softly.

Rupert expelled a long breath. It was more eloquent than words.

'Why didn't you tell me?'

He swung back to her violently, going down on one knee, his face barely inches from her own and yet hardly seeming to see her.

'How *could* I?' He struck the ground with his fist. 'How could I tell you something like that about the man you were in love with? You'd already been desperately hurt—and my hands weren't entirely clean. I'd tried to get you into bed from the first moment I set eyes on you. I'd chased you and deceived you and all but seduced you. I couldn't do that to you as well.'

Cressida stared at him in absolute disbelief. 'You thought I was in love with Keith?'

His mouth twisted. 'You don't have to be kind to me Cressida. I knew you were. Are,' he corrected himself.

'Where on earth did you get that idea?'

His eyes found her face, seemed to focus at last. In a infinitely gentle gesture he touched a finger to her lower lip

'It was obvious from the first. And in the end yo told me so, anyway.'

Cressida shook her head, the soft hair flippin against her cheek with the movement. 'I don't believ this. I *told* you so? How could I have done? When?'

Rupert smiled though his eyes were sad. 'The las time you were here.'

Cressida could not bear the sadness. 'The last time was here, I was desperately in love with you and in sucl a muddle I did not make sense, I know that. But eve so, I can't have told you I was still in love with Keith. is nonsense,' she said stringently.

He took her hand from where it lay on the grass ane carried it to his mouth where he feathered a kiss acros the knuckles.

'You're being kind again. You don't have to be. I'n a grown man. I can take the truth.'

Her heart did a little flip as she felt his lips agains her skin. She watched his down-bent head ane recognised the hollow feeling of desire deep inside hei desire and friendship and trust and the need to comfort Suddenly, nothing seemed as important as that h should know how she felt. Her fears were not gone bu they seemed feeble things compared with the love she was experiencing for him.

She turned her hand over in his, so that it was palm up to his mouth and said deliberately, 'Can you? The know that I am in love with you. Unalterably.' He raised his head, startled, his eyes questioning. She flinched but did not look away. 'For the first time in m life,' she told him.

His hold on her hand tightened almost unbearably

What?'

'I have never been in love before,' Cressida said
steadily. 'Not with Keith. Not with anyone. I should
never have married Keith, I see that now. I was much
too immature. I didn't realise how necessary love was—
or even what it was.'

His eyes were bright sea-green. 'But you said
that——' he hesitated, 'I can't remember exactly. But
that you couldn't let me make love to you because of
your memories. You know you did.' He gave their
clasped hands a little shake. 'I thought you meant that
nobody could ever replace Keith. That you would
always remember him.'

Cressida paled. 'Oh, *no*. Oh how could I?'

'It was not calculated,' Rupert told her. 'It was pure
reflex protest. That's what made it so convincing.
That's when I gave up. You can't fight that sort of
memory.'

She leaned forward and said very earnestly, 'Rupert,
my darling, when I look back on my marriage, all I can
remember is being hurt.'

He shrugged. 'That could make it more powerful.'

'No!' Her eyes filled with tears but she held on to her
composure. Somehow she had to make him know the
truth, reassure him that she was no longer Keith's.
No, listen to me. When most people look back on
relationships that have gone they remember some good
times. Don't they?' She thought of Jemima Quinn.
That's what makes them want to salvage something.'

Rupert looked faintly puzzled. 'I suppose so.'

'I didn't have any good times with Keith,' Cressida
said flatly. 'We were always strangers.'

He said softly, 'But you married him.'

She bit her lip. 'I know. I'm ashamed of that. You
won't understand.' She smiled faintly. 'Not with your
record. But I'd never been out with anyone else. Never
so much as kissed anyone else.'

Rupert made a rough, disbelieving sound.

'It's true. I was very protected when I was young. M father was terrified that some ne'er-do-well wou pursue me for my money. So he built a wall round m and—when I was obviously of marriageable age— paired me off with his heir-apparent in the business. was all done with the best of motives. But I shouldn have let it happen.'

'Were you never in love with Keith?' Rupert sa doubtfully. 'Not when you married him?'

She sighed. 'I had no idea what love was. I nev have had. I saw my future as being part of Sebastian Keith was part of Sebastians.' She shrugged. 'It ma sense in its own peculiar way.'

'But you made love with him,' Rupert said in fla voice. 'And you told me you didn't like sex. And yo wouldn't stay with me that night.'

Cressida bent her head. 'How do you think I foun out that I didn't like sex?' she asked in a low voic 'Yes, we made love. Not very often and not ver happily. That should have told me something, but didn't. I just thought I—well, that I wasn't suited to it. knew he was frustrated and I thought I was partly blame.'

He made a sharp sound as if he was hurt and dragge her against him, cradling her head against his chest he ran one hand over her hair. Cressida leaned again him thankfully. It was odd, she reflected, she ha thought that she would be able to talk to Rupert abou the things that she had always kept painfully priva but she had never really expected to do so. Now tha she had, she felt as if a great weight had been lifted o her, as if she no longer had to pretend.

Her voice muffled by his shirt, she said, 'I was afraid making love with you; I thought I would hurt you too

The stroking hand was steady, soothing. 'Hurt me But why?'

'I'd never—given satisfaction. With Keith.' She looked up at his face and saw that he was smiling tenderly. 'And you'd had so many ladies. I couldn't take the comparisons. And I thought you wanted a casual affair, like your others, and I knew I didn't. I was afraid of overloading you with emotion,' she said, absolutely honest at last.

Rupert smiled down at her. 'You make me sound like a hell-fire rake. I've never been quite the Casanova you seem to think, my love.'

'That's not what the papers say.'

'The papers say that you and I are in the middle of a steaming affair,' he pointed out. 'Which you and I know we are not.' He kissed the end of her nose. 'Yet. No, I've had previous relationships, of course. I'm thirty-seven and it is a great big liberated world out there. But not a succession of them and nothing profound.' He looked at her very seriously. 'You've got to believe this, Cress: I've made my mistakes, just as you have. I've made my bargains and some of them weren't very commendable, but I've never offered sex for love. I wouldn't do that.'

She caught her breath. 'I know,' she said softly.

'Yes. Yes, I think you do. Well, what are you going to do, Cress? It's up to you. I love you very much, you know. But if Sebastians is your whole world . . .'

'I've resigned,' she said. 'Or been sacked. I can't remember whether my father or I said it first.'

He stared at her.

'Didn't you know?' she asked, her last doubt falling away from her.

Rupert shook his head. 'It never occurred to me. I thought—well, you seemed dedicated. I thought you didn't have time for men—for me.' His mouth twisted suddenly in self-mockery. 'There was even a time when I thought *you* wanted a brief affair. It made me very angry.'

'Yes,' said Cressida, remembering their first encounters. 'Yes. I can see that. You frightened me a bit
to begin with.'

Rupert laughed softly. 'I'm glad to hear it. You
terrified *me*'.

She shook her head. 'You're joking.'

'No, I'm not. Everyone kept telling me about this
fierce executive lady who was the only one who could
keep Jerome Sebastian under control and I went and
took one look and fell for her.' His lips moved on her
hair. 'Why do you think I accepted that blindingly
unsubtle invitation of your father's? I was determined
to see you again and I didn't think you'd look twice at a
down-at-heel explorer with a half-share in a modest
travel business. You were so obviously a high-flying
executive.'

'That,' Cressida informed him, 'is drivel and you
know it. You know quite well that any sensible woman
would look twice at you.'

'Ah. I knew you were gorgeous and highly desirable
and I wanted you like mad. I didn't know you were
sensible,' Rupert pointed out wickedly.

Cressida sat up in indignation, pushing him away. He
released his hold on her. She shook her hair out and
turned to address him, to discover that she had been
outmanoeuvred. Even as she turned, he was pulling her
gently down to lie full-length beside him on the sweet-
smelling grass. With a little gasp, she fell back. Rupert
leaned over her, smiling.

'Sensible enough to know when you're beaten?' he
asked softly.

She lowered her lashes and gave a small smile. 'I
don't count myself as being beaten,' she said demurely.
'Not if you're going to kiss me, that is. It is what I have
been angling for ever since I arrived.'

'Hussy!' said Rupert.

He was laughing as he started to kiss her. It was slow

and very tantalising. Cressida let him tease her mouth for several moments. Then, with grave deliberation, she turned her head softly and began to kiss his throat while her hands drifted over his shoulders, down his spine in slow, explicit pleasure. Rupert caught his breath.

'Cress, my darling, let me make love to you. Let me show you. I'll take care of you, I promise,' he said urgently.

She was filled with joy. 'Yes, please,' she said simply.

It was, she thought in a daze, nothing like anything she had ever imagined. She had never felt so cherished, so cared for, yet at the same time so fiercely adult. She gave and demanded with equal passion and she was continually surprised at Rupert's response and her own. His hands, sometimes fierce, sometimes exquisitely tender, held her and guided her as a tornado of feeling began to build inside her. She writhed wildly, her breathing harsh, and Rupert soothed her, murmuring against her skin, implacable in his determination not to be hurried. Cressida cried out, clutching at his shoulders, surprised and almost frightened by her own sensations. He caught her wrists and held them against the grass while he slowly kissed the whole of her tense body, making her aware of her nakedness as if it were a new element. Then, and only then, did he respond to the imperative of her aching need and move inside her.

It was as if she had shed an old and over-used carapace. She felt vitally alive, new-minted, glorying in the pleasure she could give him, delighted and humbled by the way she clearly moved him; and astounded by the spiralling sensuality that filled her. When at last she clung to him, clenching and sobbing breathlessly, he wrapped his arms round her fiercely, his own body tensing as he groaned.

Afterwards, they lay in absolute peace. Eventually

Rupert moved, shifted on to his side and lay propped on one elbow watching her. She felt his fingers in her hair, spreading it fanwise over the grass. She gave a little sigh of pure satisfaction and stretched like a cat. At last her eyes drifted open. He smiled at her, his face very open and loving.

'Happy?'

'Completely,' Cressida agreed drowsily.

'Think you might give sex another chance?' he asked mischievously.

She looked reproachful. 'It's not very kind of you to laugh at me.'

'God forbid. I'm not laughing. I'm just grateful,' Rupert said soberly. 'I was afraid you might have some nasty hang-ups which would have been upsetting for both of us. Not,' he added, bending forward and kissing her mouth quickly, 'that they would have made any difference in the end.'

She reached a hand out. He received it and held it warmly.

'I didn't realise,' she said, suddenly shy. 'That it could be like that, I mean.'

'I know.'

'I'm sorry if I was stupid,' she offered.

'My darling girl, you're as entitled to muddle yourself as the rest of us, including me. And you were always generous and honest—even when you were at your most prickly. I've never loved anyone the way I love you. I never will.' Her eyes flew open. He gave a soft laugh. 'There you are, a disinterested declaration. I'm not even trying to seduce you any more.'

She smiled at him very lovingly. 'I'm impressed.'

'So you should be. I've never said that to anyone before.'

She reached out a hand and touched his chest, running her fingertips across the warm skin, tracing the line of bone and muscle with absolute confidence. She aid dreamily, 'I've never felt like this before. I didn't know one could.'

Rupert looked down at her gravely, his fingers warm round her hand.

'So what are you going to do about it?'

Cressida realised with a sense of amazement that he was hesitant, that he was no more sure of her than she had been of him. Except that now his exquisite care of her had filled her with assurance of his love. Somehow she must give him that assurance back.

She uncurled lazily, drawing him towards her.

'I think your grandmother had quite a good idea,' she murmured. He was so close now that his breath was on her lips. She smiled, arching closer, 'Will you marry me, please, Rupert?' she whispered before she lost the opportunity to say anything at all.

Harlequin *Presents*

Coming Next Month

959 THE CALL OF HOME Melinda Cross
After her father's death and her mother's recovery from her breakdown, an American painter returns to her childhood haunt to heal her own wounds—and comes up against a man who's as much in need of love as she is.

960 WOMAN OF HONOUR Emma Darcy
Labeled a home-wrecker when a certain lawyer's brother-in-law neglected to mention his marriage, an Australian chef turns workaholic. But guess who her next Dial-A-Dinner Party client is?

961 TRY TO REMEMBER Vanessa James
A distraught amnesiac and a forceful merchant banker search from Devon to Morroco for something to jolt her memory. But what really knocks her for a loop is her feelings for him.

962 A MAN POSSESSED Penny Jordan
Fate brings an old friend of a widow's late husband back into her life, the man who'd rejected her in the midst of her bleak marriage. But it seems he'd desired her, after all.

963 PASSIONATE VENGEANCE Margaret Mayo
A London designer finds herself fired on trumped-up charges. Her reputation's smeared. So the job at Warrender's Shoes seems like a lifeline—until she discovers her boss's motives in hiring her.

964 BACHELOR IN PARADISE Elizabeth Oldfield
The soap opera star a British author interviews in Florida isn't the vain celebrity she'd expected. He lives frugally, disappears every Wednesday, declares parts of his life "off-limits"—and fascinates her to no end!

965 THE ARRANGEMENT Betsy Page
Marry the woman from Maine or forfeit control of the family business, an uppercrust Bostonian warns his son. But the prospective bride is as appalled by the arrangement as the groom—so they have one thing in common, at least.

966 LOVE IN THE MOONLIGHT Lilian Peake
A young journalist wants to warn her sister in Cornwall that the man she's dallying with is a heartbreaker. But how can she—when she's still in love with the man herself?

Available in March wherever paperback books are sold, or through Harlequin Reader Service:

In the U.S.
P.O. Box 1397
Buffalo, N.Y.
14240-1397

In Canada
P.O. Box 603
Fort Erie, Ontario
L2A 5X3

Take 4 best-selling love stories FREE

Plus get a FREE surprise gift!

Special Limited-Time Offer

Mail to **Harlequin Reader Service®**

In the U.S.
901 Fuhrmann Blvd.
P.O. Box 1394
Buffalo, N.Y. 14240-1394

In Canada
P.O. Box 609
Fort Erie, Ontario
L2A 5X3

YES! Please send me 4 free Harlequin Romance® novels and my free surprise gift. Then send me 6 brand-new novels every month as they come off the presses. Bill me at the low price of $1.66 each*—a 15% saving off the retail price. There are no shipping, handling or other hidden costs. There is no minimum number of books I must purchase. I can always return a shipment and cancel at any time. Even if I never buy another book from Harlequin, the 4 free novels and the surprise gift are mine to keep forever.   116 BPR BP7S

*$1.75 in Canada plus 69¢ postage and handling per shipment.

Name _____ (PLEASE PRINT)

Address _____ Apt. No. _____

City _____ State/Prov. _____ Zip/Postal Code _____

This offer is limited to one order per household and not valid to present subscribers. Price is subject to change.   HR-SUB-1A

ATTRACTIVE, SPACE SAVING BOOK RACK

Display your most prized novels on this handsome and sturdy book rack. The hand-rubbed walnut finish will blend into your library decor with quiet elegance, providing a practical organizer for your favorite hard-or soft-covered books.

Only $9.95

Approximately 16" x 8" when assembled

Assembles in seconds

To order, rush your name, address and zip code, along with a check or money order for $10.70* ($9.95 plus 75¢ postage and handling) payable to *Harlequin Reader Service*:

Harlequin Reader Service
Book Rack Offer
901 Fuhrmann Blvd.
P.O. Box 1325
Buffalo, NY 14269-1325

Offer not available in Canada.

*New York residents add appropriate sales tax.

BKR-1R